KEY LIME KILLER

A SMALL TOWN CUPCAKE COZY MYSTERY

CUPCAKE CRIMES

MOLLY MAPLE

MARY E. TWOMEY, LLC

COPYRIGHT

DEDICATION

To starting over.

ABOUT KEY LIME KILLER

One person's trash is another person's treasure hunt... or body dump.

When Charlotte volunteers to help with the charity donation drive for the small town of Sweetwater Falls, she doesn't expect to stumble across a cookie jar whose contents hint at a foul murder. With so many items coming in for the charity drive, it's hard to tell who dropped off the incriminating evidence, and if they knew what they had.

Charlotte doesn't know what to think when all fingers point to Frank—her friend who runs the newspaper stand. Charlotte knows she doesn't have much time left if she wants to solve the murder and clear Frank's name. The cozy small town of Sweetwater Falls might have a killer on the loose, and Charlotte won't rest until she brings the guilty party to justice.

"Key Lime Killer" is filled with layered clues and cozy moments, written by Molly Maple, which is a pen name for a USA Today bestselling author.

CHARITY DRIVE MESS

*M*arianne's eyes are wide, yet I know she hasn't had a lick of caffeine this morning. "I thought the signs went up yesterday. How…"

I could finish her thought aloud, but I don't need to. How, indeed. How had a cozy small town come up with so many items to be donated in such a short time? How many items are there? My mind cannot quantify the mess, but that is exactly what we signed on to do. With Marianne's keen organizational mind and my work ethic, I didn't think we would have any problem helping to sort out the donations for the charity drive.

I clearly underestimated how much stuff the people of Sweetwater Falls want to get rid of.

There are a few enormous piles that stretch taller than my five-foot-eleven inches, and many that are wide enough to need navigational assistance to maneuver.

There are things in black garbage bags, things in small white grocery bags, and things in overflowing boxes, each stacked and toppling because more is coming in than can be organized into categories. The few volunteers that mill about seem aimless, which I completely understand. My mind is on the verge of shorting out, due to the flood of stuff.

I have no idea where to begin when I walk further into the high school gymnasium. Being that the school is closed for the summer, we have the whole space to set up some sort of organizational system for optimum shopping.

And we have less than two weeks to do it.

When the door swings open behind us, Frank shuffles inside with a large box in his arms. "Don't mind me. Just dropping off a few things for the drive."

I want to tell my friend, who is the owner and operator of the Nosy Newsy, to turn right back around. There is no way the literal mountain of clothes to my left and mish-mash of home furnishings to my right need to grow even the slightest bit taller.

Instead of bolting for the parking lot so I don't have to deal with this chaos, I wave to my great-aunt Winifred, who is busying herself sorting clothes. She looks up at me, her sea-green eyes coming into focus at my presence. "Oh, Charlotte! Just in time. I was thinking... I can't remember now. I'm in the haze." She holds her arms out as if she is a mindless mummy. Her shoulder-length silver curly hair swishes from side to side while she teeters to add to the theatrics.

My eyes are wide as I walk toward my great-aunt in all of her five-feet-tall cuteness. "This is a far larger project than I realized. Is it like this every year?"

Aunt Winifred shakes her head. "We didn't have a charity drive last year, so I think this is two years' worth of accumulated stuff. The charity drive is everyone's reminder to go through their things and get rid of what they're not using. But we didn't get that reminder last year, so it appears the drive is bursting at the seams."

Marianne balks at the madness, only she doesn't have the glazed-over look most of the volunteers wear. On the contrary, she appears enthralled, ready to tackle the challenge of a lifetime.

Thank goodness for people like Marianne.

And apparently, Rip, the Town Selectman, who loves a good event and the elbow grease that goes into it. He trots in from the hallway, blowing a whistle he's got hanging around his neck. The sound echoes through the cavernous gymnasium. "Three cheers for the new volunteers! Hip-hip!"

The lackluster "Hooray" coming from the handful of volunteers around us does not offer the intended cheer, but it's the thought that counts, I suppose.

Rip shakes his head with a goofy grin curving the corners of his mouth. He tucks his red polo shirt into his slightly pooched waistline as he jogs over to us. His salt-

and-pepper hair is firmly fixed in place with a hard shellac of hairspray. The smile on his rounded face makes him look like Santa Claus' dapper cousin, if his jolliness is any indication. "Good morning, ladies. How long do I have you for?"

Marianne had made it clear on the phone with me that she needed to sort books at noon today, so she doesn't fall behind, but after seeing the project lain out before her, she answers with a hearty, "You've got me all day, Rip. I am here for this." Her eyes are still wide, her chocolate-colored pixie-short hair swishing around her cheekbones as her head turns this way and that. She is a slight little thing, but she looks like a sturdy pioneer at the beginning of a trail she cannot wait to blaze.

My neck shrinks when I reply, "You've got me for two hours. After that, I need to get to the bakery."

Or, get *back* to the bakery, as it were. I started out my day at six this morning, baking cupcakes at the Bravery Bakery—specializing in the world's best honey cakes. It's my dream job, and being that the bakery is all mine, I can't leave my dream unattended on a whim.

Though, seeing this mammoth mess, the urge is strong to do exactly that. I don't like to leave projects unfinished, and there doesn't seem to be an end in sight for this one.

Marianne is usually my meek friend who doesn't take charge willy-nilly. But today, she looks taller, unwilling to quiet her voice when she knows it is useful. "I'm thinking you need someone in charge of sorting the household items." She motions to the far-left wall. "We need tables up first, so we can set the things where they'll need to go instead of shuffling them around in piles. Also, we'll need more real estate. What do you think about collapsing the bleachers to make more room for tables?"

Rip scratches his head, turning to survey the bleachers. "Where would people sit while they eat their hot dogs?"

Of course this isn't just a simple charity drive. There will be a picnic lunch and live music. Rip doesn't do things halfway.

Marianne jerks her thumb to the exit. "Can we move the food outside and set up picnic blankets instead of using the bleachers?"

He clasps his hands together, impossibly more cheerful at her suggestion. "A citywide picnic? That sounds like the best idea I've ever heard! And picnic blankets instead of tables and chairs will be far easier to set up and tear down. I love it!"

Marianne nods once. "Sounds good. Where are the long tables, Rip?"

Rip laughs like a man who appreciates the simple joys in life as he throws his arms around Marianne. "I'm so glad you're here. Yes, that's fantastic. If you like, you can help me bring out the long tables and get them set up. Then I'm turning you loose on household items. No one seems to want to tackle that this morning."

Marianne cracks her knuckles like a boxer gearing up

for the match of a lifetime. "I've got this, Rip. But I'm keeping Charlotte with me. I'll need a helper."

Rip salutes Marianne, and I love everything about the exchange—especially that I don't have to make decisions about what needs to happen first. It's all a jumbled mess to me.

Marianne points in Aunt Winnie's direction. "The clothing sorters need to each take a bag and sort the contents into the various piles. I see they're just searching for one category of clothing and leaving the rest. That means each bag will be gone through four times (men's, women's, children's, and bedding). Unnecessary."

Rip holds up his finger enthusiastically. "On it! I'll redirect the clothing volunteers. Charlotte, can you help Marianne with the tables?"

I nod, and Rip trots off to the clothing area. "You know, Rip is one of a kind. He's happy to take charge and happy to let others call the shots if they can do it better."

"Oh, he's fantastic." Marianne motions to the hallway. "Let's get cracking. If I've got you for two hours, I want every bit of work you've got until you walk out that door."

I salute her because I love the idea of not being in charge for two whole hours. I'm not naturally an assertive person, so being the decisionmaker for my business stretches a muscle I didn't realize I had at the ready. When I can give that muscle a rest and just be the employee, it is a relief I will not push aside.

Marianne and I make quick work of setting up a row of

long rectangular tables that stretch from the front of the gymnasium to the back. It's probably not a good sign that I am already sweating, but I keep my grunts and groans silent, so as not to dampen Marianne's forward motion. She grabs up Rip's abandoned clipboard and tears a few sheets from his notepad, scribbling on them before she makes her way to the row of tables. "Here," she says, taping a paper to one table, then moving to the next. "These are the categories, labeled so we don't get confused. Start with one box and don't put it down until it's been emptied. If you're not sure where it should go, set it on the Miscellaneous table, but let's not get precious about the piles. Guessing wrong is fine. We don't want the Miscellaneous table overflowing by the end." When she catches me eyeing the avalanche of items to sort, she puts herself in my eyeline. "Focus on one box at a time, otherwise we'll get overwhelmed."

Marianne is usually my sweet, softspoken bestie, but today she is large and in charge. I love it, so I don't waste a second before I comply with her orders.

"On it!" I sing, pretending I am not daunted by this task in the least. I pick up the nearest box, uncertain what a few of the items that greet me actually are. But Marianne's words ring in my head that it's better to guess wrong than to dawdle over getting everything perfect.

Tin kettle.

Cast-iron skillet half-covered in rust.

Salt and pepper shakers.

Plastic planters.

I sort everything as quick as I can onto the tables that Marianne was smart enough to label. She used vague enough specifications that I don't hem and haw over finding an overly specific category.

Man, she's good.

Marianne ignores her phone when it rings, keeping her eyes on her task as though it is the only thing in her mind. She is a tiny machine, but powerful and unstoppable. Her work ethic puts a fire under me, and in turn, the rest of the volunteers pick up their pace, as well.

Three boxes are broken down and thrown into the garbage bin. Four. When I hit my fifth, I feel as though I have found my rhythm as I unpack the items and set them on their respective tables.

Dull kitchen knives.

Black kitchen towels.

Baseball.

Wire cutters.

Cookie jar.

The kitchen hardware items should go to my right, so I sort the other items first, and then head to the end of the row with the dull knives and the cookie jar.

I don't expect the mountain of clothing to tumble in my direction, nor do I anticipate how cumbersome the avalanche might be when it doesn't stop and refuses to make room for my steps. A volunteer shrieks an apology to the rest of us as the mountain topples, but I can't get out of the way fast enough.

The kitchen knives and the cookie jar fly from my hands when I am pushed sideways by a snowman-sized bundle of clothing. I cringe and shout a quick, "Heads up!" scrambling to get out of the way as the knives and jar fling upward and then come crashing to the ground.

"Ah!" I grimace, shocked that I couldn't get out of there fast enough to avoid one of the knives nicking my forearm. The cookie jar crashes to the ground, shattering into pieces, and the rest of the knives stake themselves into various garments that are puddled at my feet.

Marianne gasps and runs to me, tugging me toward the tables and away from the mess that I partially created. "Oh, Charlotte! You're bleeding!"

"It's fine," I tell her, inspecting the outside of my arm. In truth, the cut doesn't seem particularly deep, but the shock of it is still ringing through me. "The knives are scattered on the ground, though. I need to clean that up, so no one gets hurt."

Marianne types out a text on her phone. "Logan is going to take you to Urgent Care."

"I'm really okay."

My best friend isn't one to take chances with my health. "One of those knives cut you? That wound needs to be cleaned out by a professional. No arguments."

"But I only sorted a few boxes! I can do more."

Marianne eyes me, her hand on her hip while she

waits for a reply text from my boyfriend. "I'm sure you can, after you go to Urgent Care, and they make sure you're not going to get an infection from the knife that cut you."

I roll my eyes like a child being told to take their medicine. "Oh, fine. At least let me clean up the mess so no one else gets hurt."

Marianne takes a handful of tissues from the package in her purse and presses them to my arm. "Okay, but that's the last thing you're doing. Then you're sitting way over there and waiting for Logan."

"I can drive myself."

Her phone chirps with a text. She straightens her posture as she exercises her authority. "You can prove that after your arm has been looked at by a medical professional."

I grumble just loud enough for her to hear that I am unhappy at leaving her to deal with the project as I make my way to the dropped knives and smashed cookie jar. I pick up the knives, though I am uncertain how many there were, so I do a thorough job of searching the pile to make sure no one has the misfortune of stepping on one if they pass by this area. My fingers are slippery as blood dribbles down my forearm and tickles my hand.

Perhaps the cut is deeper than I realized.

It's when I lift an orange dress to search it for the strewn cutlery that my movements still. I blink twice, unable to make sense of what my mind is telling me I am seeing.

"That's got to be a Halloween prop," I murmur to myself as I reach down and pick up the severed hand that looks like it belonged to a woman. It has to be the best faked appendage I've ever seen in my life, wrapped in plastic. But the second my fingers uncurl the digits of the strange item, my spine stiffens. I know what rubber props feel like, and this is not that. The skin gives, and there is bruising around the wrist where tendons and sinew stretch out like spaghetti inside the plastic.

My intake of breath is enough for Marianne to rush to my side. "You shouldn't be bothering with this, Charlotte. I'll clean up the..." But when she sees the same thing that's sent my heart rate into overdrive, I know that Marianne is rethinking her choice to volunteer at the charity drive this morning.

I turn to my best friend, eyes wide and spine tingling with the unknown. "Marianne, you need to call the police. I think there's been a murder."

2

HANDY DONATION

*O*n a normal day, the police wouldn't have a problem getting into the gymnasium, but today, it is madness trying to show them where the severed hand lies. When the clothing mountain topples a second time, I hold my ground, pushing the garments off as fast as I can, so nothing lands on the evidence.

I don't know how to keep the area clear without possibly getting my blood on things, so Marianne remains by my side, shoving old sweatpants out of the way while we guard the hand until the police can get to us. The cut on my forearm has seeped through the tissues Marianne gave me. That, paired with holding what I wish was a prop from a horror movie, makes me look truly unhinged.

Logan is first on the scene, because Marianne had already called him to come and take me to Urgent Care when one of the dull knives cut my arm. His partner, Wayne, and his father, Sheriff Flowers, aren't far behind. Logan is in his uniform, looking like a superhero come to life with his sandy blond hair and Superman chin dimple. He wades through the clothes, but to me he looks like a lifeguard coming to our rescue, weathering the storm to ensure our safety.

I might have an over-the-top crush on my boyfriend, which doesn't seem to be fading anytime soon. "Careful, Logan!" I warn him when he gets too near a giant pile of sweaters. Luckily, he holds up his hands and stops the landslide before the whole thing topples him, but it's a close call. "Go the other side of the tables," I instruct him. "Walk along the bleachers, or you're likely to make more clothes fall near the evidence."

Logan frowns at us. "Evidence? What do you mean? I thought I was here to take you to a doctor because you cut yourself."

Marianne speaks up. "I called the precinct after I texted you. Charlotte found a severed hand inside a cookie jar! It smashed, and we're trying not to move the hand or let it get crushed by all the clothes."

Logan races to the other side of the tables, taking my advice and rushing along the bleachers to avoid another clothing catastrophe. "Are you serious?" When his father and his partner come further into the gymnasium, he waves them over, showing them the safer path they should take. "Charlotte, are you okay?"

He is ever the perfect man, caring more about my well-being than the job he loves.

I nod, holding up my arm that has a handful of bloody tissues stuck to it. "I'm alright. I can take myself to Urgent Care. I think the severed hand is more of a priority at the moment."

Marianne hisses at my phrasing. "I'll drive you, and I'll make sure the doctor knows what happened, so you are properly cared for."

Aunt Winnie calls from the other side of the mountain. "I can take her! Charlotte, I'm coming!"

"Stay over there, Aunt Winnie! There's broken shards on the ground over here. I'll come that way in a minute."

Marianne steadies me when I nearly slip and fall on a silky nightgown. "Logan, what do you need from us?"

Logan runs his hand over his face. "Your statements, for starters. Tell me everything. Point me to the donor who gifted this lovely item to the charity drive. I don't suppose you all took down the names and wrote them on the bags and boxes belonging to each person, did you?"

Marianne is flustered, huffing while she looks around helplessly. "Were we supposed to do that?"

Logan shakes his head, fixing her with a good-natured half-smile. "No. But that would have made finding the person who offloaded a human hand a whole lot easier." He motions to the mess. "Can you tell me what else was in the box? Or was it just the cookie jar with the hand inside?"

I jerk my chin to the knives in my grip. "These knives, that dish towel, a baseball and wire cutters. The box is..." I cast around until my gaze falls on an empty cardboard container near a table. "That's the box."

Logan nods, explaining things to his father and Wayne when they finally make their way to the spot. After they take their turns questioning me, Logan helps Marianne and me away from the crime scene, but not before we are sure the clothes won't topple the moment we step away. He takes the knives I've collected and hands them to his father, so Sheriff Flowers can mark them as evidence and keep them separate from the rest of the stuff.

Logan's hugs are the best, though he's up against steep competition. Sweetwater Falls is a city of huggers. I am never more than a few steps away from someone who has a warm embrace at the ready. But Logan's firm chest and his spicy, floral pine scent push out a portion of my stress, like air being deflated from an overfull balloon. While his father and his partner take pictures and do their best to rope off the crime scene, Logan's hand rubs a soothing circle on my back. "You cut yourself."

"With a used knife," Marianne chimes in. "No idea how clean it was. If it was the same knife that was used to cut off this person's hand..." When my eyes squinch shut at the thought, Marianne links her littlest finger around mine. "I'm sure it's going to heal just fine. But I'll feel better once a doctor takes a look at it."

Logan fixes me with an expression of mild frustration

when he pulls back. "I want to take you to the doctor, but I have to be here to help with the investigation."

I reach up and kiss his cheek. "It's just a small cut. I'm fine. Whoever did this was brazen enough to try to hide the evidence in plain sight in here. They need to be brought to justice. You stay here and do the job you're so good at." Logan insists on helping me to the exit with one arm around my waist and the other pressing the bloody tissues to my arm. When Marianne reaches for her purse on the way, I frown at her. "No way. I can drive just fine. You stay here, where you're needed. Rip will cry if he loses his best volunteer."

Marianne's stubborn nature usually only sees the light of day when it's to protect the people she loves, and this is no exception. "Not a chance. I'm going with you."

"I'll let you talk to the doctor on the phone. You stay. Both of you. Can you drive Aunt Winnie home after this? I was going to take her home myself."

Marianne salutes me. "On it, but you're not going alone. Frank!"

I would have thought Frank left after dropping off his box of donations, but apparently he either had more to donate, or he got caught up in conversation and didn't make a quick exit. He's a chatty one, so either option is entirely plausible.

Frank nods to us. "What's the good word, kids? What are the police doing here? I was just about to drive off when I saw a squad car pull in."

Marianne doesn't answer his question, but hands me over to Frank, as if I am prone to fainting or something. "Charlotte cut her arm on a used knife. Could you take her to Urgent Care and see that she makes it home safely?"

I cringe that she thinks I am not sturdy enough to look after myself. "I'm really fine."

Frank smiles at Marianne as if I haven't spoken, showing off his missing front tooth. "Of course! Hop into my truck, Cupcake Queen. I've got you."

Marianne and Logan don't look the slightest bit put off by the glower I cast them both, as if they've conspired to make me look as feeble as possible to my friend.

I walk with Frank to his truck, recalling that on any given day, Frank can fill up enough of a conversation to make the thing a monologue. He runs the newsstand in town, plus he is dating Delia, the town gossip, so he can take up whole hours with nonstop chatter

I settle into the passenger's seat of his old truck that looks to have more rust on it than is structurally sound.

Frank immediately turns the conversation to me. "What did I miss back there? The police didn't show up because you got a cut on your arm."

I relay the highlights to Frank since that's all I have. "It's a good thing they're there now. I wouldn't know the first thing about where to start with an investigation like that. It's like searching for a needle in a haystack."

Frank's motor is loud as he drives me toward Urgent Care. "Aw, it's not as hopeless as that. Even if we don't know who sent in the severed hand, the police will do their tests and figure out whose hand that is. Then we can work our way back from there, fishing out who might have had a reason to cut off the hand of the person in question."

I press my lips together, pondering his logic. "I suppose that makes sense. But the hand didn't look all that fresh." I wince at my phrasing. "I mean, it was lumpy in spots and bruised. I'm not sure they'll be able to identify who it came from quite that easily."

Frank gives a thoughtful, "Hmm." When he turns onto the next street, he tries a different line of reasoning. "We'll have to see if anyone's neighbors have gone missing. The charity drive is a good place to do a loose headcount." He shakes his head. "I wish Delia was here. She knows everything about everyone. She would know who's missing and who might have done something like this."

I turn my head to him. "Delia's still visiting her mom?"

Frank nods. "She's been there two weeks, and I can't say I'm thrilled at the distance. I know it's good for Delia to stay with her mom every now and then, but her mother lives several hours from here, so it's not exactly a day trip." He waves his hand to clear the air of his words. "I'm whining. Can't fault a man in love for missing his woman, I suppose. On the phone, I'm all supportive. 'Good that you're staying an extra week. Your mother misses you.' But in my heart, I miss my sweet Delia."

I love that Frank is ever smitten with the flighty town gossip. It was the cutest thing to watch them begin to date, and now to be in a full-blown relationship. Frank is probably the only person in town who thinks the occasionally prickly woman is sweet. It's good they found each other.

I wince when I see I've bled through the tissues and have a few droplets dotting my shorts. "Got any napkins, Frank? I don't want to get blood on your car."

Frank nods, so I reach into the glovebox, assuming that's where they're kept, but Frank gives a harried, "No! Not in there!"

The glovebox was filled to capacity, apparently, and the second it pops open, a litany of maps, papers, garbage, travel-sized condiments and something heavy and silver fills my lap and the floor of the truck. Like scarves from a clown's sleeve, the clutter keeps on coming.

The heavy silver thing slides down my leg, but I feel it tear across my shin. "Ow! Oh! I'm sorry, Frank. I'll get it all back in."

Frank shakes his head. "I'll take care of it. Just push it all to the floor." He pops open the center console and hands me two brown napkins. "Here. Take these."

"My leg is bleeding, I think. What is that?"

Frank sighs, pulling the truck into the parking lot of the Urgent Care, which is just outside the city proper. "It's for emergencies."

"Something cut me." I feel the wetness on my shin. "Well, it's a good thing we're at Urgent Care."

Frank comes around to my side and opens the door for me. If I do it myself, the papers and garbage will go fluttering all over the parking lot. He winces when he helps me down from the truck. "That looks deep, Cupcake Queen."

I glance at the blood that trails down my leg and begins to stain my sock. "What was in there, Frank?"

He reaches into the clutter and pulls out a hunting knife that's come loose from its sheath. "Sorry about that. It's supposed to latch closed, but the snap here broke off last week."

"I didn't know you hunted."

Frank's neck shrinks. "That's because I'm not very good at it. I get together with a few guys every now and then and head off to the woods to try my hand at being a wilderness master. A bit of hunting and fishing. I usually end up with a bad case of poison ivy and a serious appreciation for indoor plumbing. Last week, all I caught was a fish too small to keep."

I chuckle at his honesty. "That sounds about right. Who do you go with?"

"Rip and Bill. We like to pretend we're born for the great outdoors. Good for the ego at first but after two days without a proper mattress, it's a kick to the ego."

"That's quite the double-edged sword."

"Speaking of swords," he says, motioning to my leg. "Let's get you in to a doctor who can patch you up. You're an accident magnet today, it seems, and that was the last of my napkins."

I can walk just fine, but Frank offers his arm like a

gentleman. His slicked-back oily black hair falls forward when he reaches down to shove some of the scattered papers back into his truck to deal with later. I catch sight of a takeout bag from a restaurant I've never heard of. "What's The Funky Chicken? Is that around here?"

Frank shoves the bag into his pocket, I assume to throw into the trash on our way inside. "Oh, nothing. Just a place that sells all-you-can-eat chicken dinners near Evansville."

My nose scrunches. "Where's Evansville? Is that around here?"

Frank's neck shrinks. "No. It's where Delia's mom lives. She left her cell phone charger at her house, so I drove it up to her."

I balk at Frank's thoughtfulness. "Are you serious? How far away is that?"

"Four hours. It was worth it, though. I got to meet Delia's mom." He straightens, looking proud of himself for crossing such an important relationship marker. "She called me a sweet man when I met them at the restaurant."

"Well, she got it spot on. That sounds like a rave review from the future mother-in-law."

Frank runs his free hand through his greasy hair. "Can you imagine? Me with a mother-in-law? I never thought someone like Delia would say yes to a date with me, and now I've met her mother." Frank beams with happiness, and I reckon relational bliss couldn't have happened to a more deserving person. "Took my two ladies out to eat, then headed back home."

I'm a little miffed that Delia didn't just run to the nearest store and buy a replacement charger, instead asking Frank to drive four hours to bring her one, but if Frank is okay with it, then I suppose the good friend thing to do is let him enjoy the ride.

Frank opens the door for me, ushering me inside. He helps me fill out the paperwork because, while my arm is nearly clotted, it still needs pressure applied. He asks me all the questions needed, which aren't terribly embarrassing, but are a bit more personal than the two of us usually are. He doesn't know my parents' names. He doesn't know my medical history, which gratefully, isn't all that much to jot down.

"Occupation?" he asks, and then snickers to himself. "Just kidding. *Cupcake Queen*."

I snort at him. "You didn't seriously write that, did you?"

He turns the clipboard to me with a mischievous grin, showing me that he indeed wrote that on my form.

I kind of love it. Gratitude swells in my heart at the simple joke that only comes when you have friends who know you well enough to poke at your sense of humor. I never had that when I lived in the big city before I moved here. I didn't let people know me, not because I was jaded or didn't want to let people in. I didn't know how to invite strangers into my life and turn them into friends. Life is different in Sweetwater Falls. Here, even someone like me —shy to the point of forgetting the sound of my own voice

—can find friends who know exactly how to bring about a laugh.

Frank motions to my expression with his pen. "What's that look for? You were laughing, but now you look like you're about to start singing one of those heart-wrenching songs that make me want to adopt a three-legged dog."

I smile at his phrasing. "I was just thinking how glad I am that I moved to Sweetwater Falls. Thinking how lucky I am to have a friend to drive me to Urgent Care."

"Feeling lucky, even though you've got blood dripping down your leg from my camping knife?" He clucks his tongue. "You're something else, Charlotte McKay."

I bump my shoulder to his. "So long as I'm in Sweetwater Falls, I'm happy. It's the people that make the place special."

Frank pulls me into a one-armed hug so he can muss my strawberry blonde curls with the affection of an older cousin being sweet to his younger cousin. Even though we are not related, I feel the closeness of what it is to have a friend, and how valuable a treasure that has turned out to be.

3

CAMPING TRIP

$\mathcal{I}$'m not a fan of getting stitches, it turns out. But after the cut on my arm was cleaned properly, my blood tested for any scary things that might have been embedded in the blade that cut me, and the injury closed, I am grateful for the doctor who is just as good at his job as I am at making cupcakes, which is no small praise.

Frank cleaned out his glovebox while I was being treated, so the drive back to the high school gymnasium where I left my car was not spent wading through his piles of paper and trash, thank goodness.

Marianne is in her zone. I can tell just by watching her supreme focus while she tears through a bag of donations and sorts them with the fervor of someone who just arrived on the scene, not showing the least bit of wear, that the hours of work have not dampened her spirit in the least. When I flag her down, she pauses to throw her arms around me. "Oh, Charlotte! I was so worried! What did the doctor say?"

I smile at her fretting. "That I'll live to sort another box. I've got ten minutes before I have to head back to the bakery. Put me to work, chief."

Marianne motions to the mountain of clothing that now looks like a large hill, thanks to all the work the volunteers have put into the task. "I took Winnie home not too long ago. She was looking a little tired. And Rip and I put a stop to any more donations for the day, so we can get a handle on what we've got here." She motions to the spot where the hand was discovered. "The crime scene was so chaotic that they had to take the hand and the things surrounding it back to the precinct, which means we can keep working. Good thing, right? I can't imagine losing a whole day if they'd had to shut the place down."

Gotta love Marianne when she's on a mission.

I head over to the household items and pick up where I left off, waving goodbye to Frank, who doesn't waste a second getting back to his newsstand so he can make up for lost time. My arm is stiff while I take old plates out of boxes and place them on the appropriate table, but I keep my steady pace while the other volunteers bustle around me.

When Rip sidles up next to me, his hand on my shoulder is gentle, as if I am fragile and might fall over at the first sign of a stiff breeze. "You alright, kiddo?"

I set down a stack of cups, taking out the one that is

chipped so it can be discarded. "It was a dramatic scratch, is all. I'm more worried about the person whose hand ended up in a cookie jar. Frank suggested we should do some sort of headcount at the fair to make sure everyone in the city is accounted for. How possible do you think that might be?"

Rip thumbs his rounded chin. "I'm not sure. Can't be impossible. I can make that happen. The trouble is, not everyone has to come to the fair. Just because someone doesn't show doesn't mean they are dead."

My mouth pulls to the side while I take in his very logical addendum. "True enough. I'm just trying to think how we might be able to find the person whom the hand belongs to."

Rip picks up a heavy pot and sets it on the table for me. "I think we might have to leave this one to the professionals. As much as I wish there was a quick solution, criminal actions don't come with flashing neon signs."

"If only."

Rip chortles as he tugs a fishing pole out of the stack, doing his best to untangle it from the web of clothing without sticking the hook into his thumb by mistake. "This isn't a bad fishing pole, if you ask me. I might set this aside to buy when the charity drive begins. You know that, as a volunteer, we get first pick of the donations to buy."

"I didn't know that. If I see something I'd like to buy, I'll put it next to your fishing pole." I set a stack of candle holders on the table. "Do you do much fishing?"

Rip sighs like the romantic he is. "Not as much as I would like to. I haven't been camping in far too long, which is usually when I break out the old fishing pole. I go with Frank and Bill a few times throughout the summer, but we haven't made the time to get out there in nature this summer yet. Must remedy."

I frown when something odd clicks in my mind. "Wait, what? Frank mentioned going hunting and fishing with you and Bill just last week."

Rip shakes his head. "Unless there's a second Rip around here, that's not accurate. Maybe Frank was thinking of this time last year?"

"Probably." But I know that's not it. Frank mentioned that he goes out on his wilderness adventures with Rip and Bill, and that he just went last week. Why would Frank lie about being out with Bill and Rip camping when he wasn't? My eyebrows bunch as the timer on my phone rings, reminding me that I need to get back to the cupcakery if I want to finish my orders in time for the weekly pick-ups.

I wave goodbye to Marianne and Rip, wishing I could drill down more details of the camping trip that never happened, but Rip meanders off to help the next volunteer with a stack of clothing bigger than her body.

I want to leave this investigation to the professionals. I should push the crime out of my mind and trust that people more qualified than me will put their heads together and find the person who did this.

But as I walk to my car in the midday sunshine, I know that while my hands might find their purpose frosting cupcakes, my mind will be occupied with the fragmented clues of a murder investigation for the foreseeable future.

4

BETTY'S HONEYMOON

*B*etty is a welcome sight when I get to the cupcakery, which is the well cared for commercial kitchen in the back of Sweetwater Fountains. My sole paid employee works as if I am paying her a hundred dollars an hour for top effort, when we both know her hourly wage falls far short of what someone so skilled at assisting in a kitchen deserves. "Hi, sweetheart. Oh, what happened to your arm?"

I hold up the bandaged forearm with a sulky expression. "Hazards of volunteering for the charity drive." I explain to her the dramatic lows of the morning, taking in her gasps of horror while she listens with rapt attention. Her blonde-white hair is pinned back to show off each nuance of her shock. By the end of my account, she is paler than her cream jogging suit.

She presses her hands to her cheeks. "That is terrifying! Who would do such a thing? And then who would donate the cookie jar? That's sick. This whole thing. I don't want to believe anyone could be so horrible, or so foolish." She shakes her head as she sits on the sole stool in the place. "Why not dispose of the hand where no one could find it? Why donate it where someone is sure to buy it and discover what's inside?"

I shrug. "None of it makes sense to me, but I suppose that's a good thing—that murder doesn't seem logical to us. If it did, we might have a serious problem on our hands."

Betty chortles. "True, true." Then she motions to the counter where the wire racks are lined up in a neat row that stretches the length of the stainless steel. "I finished baking the vanilla latte cupcakes, and I'm just about to pull out the last of the vanilla bean cupcakes."

"Did I ever tell you you're amazing? An absolute godsend? An angel of mercy?"

Betty fans herself at my compliments. "You forgot bombshell."

I incline my head in silent apology to her at the oversight. "Absolutely."

Betty frowns at the rows of cupcakes that have just finished cooling. "Are you sure you don't need me to stay a few more hours? I feel bad, leaving you with so much work still left to do."

I shrug at what doesn't seem like a daunting task in the least, given that before Betty, I didn't have part-time help, apart from Logan and Marianne, who lent a hand whenever they could. "All I have to do is frost them. I finished baking the double-fudge cupcakes this morning. It's your anniversary lunch today, right? You've got plans with your hubby. You don't want to skip that."

Betty's head bobs. "Sure, but you've also got to come up with a flavor of the month and bake those. You've only got two days to dream up a recipe, perfect it, and then bake truckloads of it. I'm not sure you want to look at how many orders have been placed for the cupcake of the month."

I grimace at the very legitimate setback, but just as quickly, I brush off the decision I've been avoiding by shifting the conversation to Betty as she begins taking out the trays of vanilla bean cupcakes from the oven. "Where did you and Rip go on your honeymoon? Tell me it was somewhere that didn't have severed hands in cookie jars."

Betty chuckles. "Oh, nowhere fancy, but I suppose fanciness isn't always the point of romantic times for a young couple. We went to a city not too far from here. Apple Blossom Bay is a small town on the water. We rented a cottage near the beach, walked holding hands on the shore every night and spent our time being in love with no distractions. Money was quite the issue back then. I was only twenty-one years old, mind you."

A small smile finds me when I didn't think anything would soothe my nerves today. That's the magic of Betty, I guess. "Where would you have gone, had money been no object?"

Betty's sigh is a contented one, and I love the sound of it on her. "Honestly? Probably exactly there all over again. That same seaside small town. That same cottage. That same beach. It's a beautiful setting and the company never disappoints. It's the company that makes or breaks a honeymoon."

I love that Betty is a romantic. I love that someone who works as hard for our small town as Rip has an angel in his corner who is hopelessly in love with him.

"Tell me about your honeymoon," I say to Betty. "The G-rated parts."

She takes out two more trays from the oven while a far-off smile crinkles the corners of her hazel eyes. "I will once you start sketching the cupcake of the month."

"You're strict." But when I fetch my sketch pad and a pencil, I realize this is exactly the sort of distraction I need to get my mind off the crime I stumbled upon this morning.

Betty waits until my pencil begins jotting down notes. "It was forty-nine years ago, you realize. For me to be able to pick out details is a miracle in and of itself. It means they mattered enough to hold onto after all these years."

I wait out her stalling, and finally, I am rewarded with the romance of two people who have managed to keep their love afloat for nearly half a century.

"Rip has always been a planner. He planned everything about the proposal. He even had my mother make my favorite dessert to celebrate—key lime pie with extra graham cracker crumbles on top. Too tart, just how I like it. It's not a key lime pie if your lips don't pucker." She imitates the sour face before continuing. "So, it was a shocker when for the honeymoon, Rip wanted no plans. He wanted two weeks of nothing but the beach and me, as he put it." Her cheeks color, and I love the sight of the girlishness on her features. "It was simple, but perfect—which is how we've lived our lives ever since."

"Simple but perfect?" I echo, a wistful happiness settling in the sugary air of the bakery.

"That's exactly right. We had dessert for breakfast and woke up at noon. We rented a boat and went fishing when we were hungry and lounged away the two weeks. Simple but perfect."

"I really love that."

Betty turns on the music as her generous hips sway to the classic songs of her youth. "Don't worry, Charlotte. The flavor of the month will come to you. Until it does, make sure that your next date with that handsome police officer of yours is simple but perfect. Those are the best moments. You don't want to miss them."

I press my lips together as thoughts of Logan cloud out the unsolved mystery of the severed hand, and the unsettled feeling that accompanies such a puzzle.

As I let go of my frustration, my pencil falls to the paper, sketching out a cupcake I know Betty will love.

5

LOVE AND LOGAN

*A*fter baking all afternoon and experiencing quite a few missteps, I finally landed on a cupcake that was equally fluffy as it was delicious. The citrus fragrance permeated my nose for so many hours that I began to crave any other scent. Plus, I'd gone over the possibilities of who could have done something so horrible as to donate a severed hand to charity so many times that I decided I needed a break. Betty had been right, though, that the cupcake orders for the flavor of the month were stacked high and required quite a bit of elbow grease to fulfill. Hundreds of warm cupcakes were cooling on racks atop my counter, but even that accomplishment couldn't bust me of the delusion that I might somehow solve this mystery if only I obsess about it enough.

I shake my head at myself, turning to my goldfish that swishes her tail in her bowl atop my counter. "What do you think, Buttercream? I'm sure it doesn't mean anything that Frank said he was fishing with Bill and Rip, yet Rip told me he hadn't been fishing himself recently. Maybe Frank got his dates mixed up and was remembering the last time they went as being more recent."

Buttercream flicks her tail at my flimsy hypothesis.

"I know. That sounded implausible when I said it. Still, I like Frank. He's a good guy. I can't believe he would knowingly hurt anyone."

My mind plays devil's advocate, reminding me that Frank was there, dropping off donations when I arrived. So, he was at the scene of the crime.

I answer my traitorous mind aloud, directing my words at my elegant goldfish. "That hardly proves anything. Loads of people were in and out of the high school gymnasium. That's where the donations were supposed to be left. That doesn't make him the killer."

"What doesn't make who the killer?"

When the male voice answers me, I shriek at the second non-fish presence, whirling around with a dirty spatula in hand, ready to defend my territory, if need be.

My boyfriend's hands raise, surrendering to the oncoming assault with a kitchen utensil. "It's just me!"

"Logan!" I lower the spatula with my exhale. "I didn't know you were coming here." I set down the last of the dirty dishes in the sink and close the gap between us, throwing my sweaty arms around his sturdy shoulders.

I can hear Logan's smile in his reply. "Hey, you.

Thought I'd surprise my favorite girl. Had a long day at work. Wondered if I could take you out to dinner."

Elation spreads through me as I hug him tighter. "That's very thoughtful. And perfect timing. I just finished baking, and these need to cool before they can be frosted."

His arm remains around my waist as he peers around me to take in the large scale of cupcakes dotting the counter. "Wow! Charlotte, are those all the flavor of the month?"

I nod while his thumb rubs a spot just above my hips. The small motion sends a wave of calm through me. He's like a magician, what with the way he shows up at the exact right time, so I don't have to pause my baking, and then soothes me when my mind is spinning out. "It's been a long day, but they turned out how I wanted, so I'm happy."

Logan presses a light kiss to the tip of my nose just to be cute. "Sounds like you could use a wrist massage—both before and after you do all the icing work."

I bury my face in his green polo shirt. "Stop saying the perfect thing. It's making me fall more hopelessly for you."

Logan's chuckle is a beautiful sound that moves his chest and warms my heart. "Can't have that." Logan stares into my eyes, and I can tell he's taking a moment to appreciate the quiet and the togetherness that doesn't come as often as either of us would like when there is a murder investigation afoot. He takes his time examining my features, as if he hasn't seen me in weeks, and wants to admire me anew.

There's something different about him this evening—a tenderness in the way he regards me. Maybe it's that he looks fresh from a shower—shaved and smelling like the best kind of hug a girl can ask for. I can't put my finger on what it is that seems to have shifted his demeanor.

I can tell he's been stuck in his head for too long and needs to get something off his chest before he can enjoy our impromptu date. "What's on your mind, Logan?"

Of course, I know what's on his mind. He's a police officer in a town where their local baker found a severed hand in a random cookie jar. But it's the invitation he deserves to hear, and I hope it opens him up to be able to unload his stress, if that's what he needs.

Logan gathers a long breath into his lungs, his hands moving to cup my cheeks. "Charlotte, I love you." Then the instant the words leave his mouth, he squinches his eyes shut and winces. "Oh, man!"

Wonder and confusion fight for first place on my face. "You love me?" Everything in me feels lighter, including my aching feet that just moments ago were weighing me down.

Logan steps back, scrubbing his hands over his face as if he'd like to erase those three words from my memory. "Yes, but I wasn't supposed to blurt it out like that! I had a plan. I was going to take you to a nice restaurant with cloth napkins and a menu that doesn't have French fries on it. I had a whole speech prepared, too. I was going to tell you how lucky I am to have found you. That I'm sorry your time in Chicago didn't pan out, but I'm glad it didn't, because it led you here." Logan throws his head back, addressing the ceiling instead of my astonishment. "I was going to tell you that I've never felt this way about anyone before, and that you're it for me." He motions to my face. "But one look at you with cupcake batter smeared across your forehead, and I blurt it out like a fool with no plan. You're the kind of woman who deserves a plan, and I know that! I know I'm the lucky one."

Logan rarely spins out like this, so I do my best to rein him back in. This time, it's my turn to cup his cheeks in my hands and examine his gorgeous features up close. His eyes shut tight, as if he cannot withstand the blatant embarrassment of going off-book.

"Logan, look at me."

When he refuses, it's my turn to kiss his nose. His shoulders lower, but I can tell he is still upset with himself.

So silly. Up close like this, I can drink in the details of the man I adore. He is freshly shaved, and I can smell his cologne. His sandy blond hair isn't mussed in the slightest. I can tell he went home from work and took a shower before coming here, thinking through all the details to profess his love as seamlessly as possible.

I've never told a man I loved him before, but now that it's here, I know what it feels like. "I'm the lucky one," I tell him, though I know these aren't the perfect words, even if they are true. "Sometimes I still can't believe my good fortune that I found you—that you gave me a second look. You're the most beautiful, thoughtful man I've ever known in real life." I take a chance and lean in to press a chaste kiss to his full lips. "Of course I love you, Logan."

At this declaration of what I thought should be obvious by now, Logan's eyes fly open in astonishment. "You do?"

Between my smile and his, I'm fairly certain we could light up a football field with how much joy sparks between us in the middle of this moment that Logan wasn't sure would land. Moisture dots my lashes when I blink. My heart swells to near bursting, appreciating anew the day I had no idea would end like this.

6

SUSPECTS AND SWEET NOTHINGS

*W*hen Logan plans something, he doesn't go halfway. The date he set up is at a restaurant in Hamshire. The place isn't so fancy that I don't feel as if I can't come straight from work, but it also doesn't have the hometown, casual feel to it. He called ahead and made reservations for us. I'm sure that's a very normal thing that most women are accustomed to, but Logan is my first serious boyfriend, so even the little things like that feel like their own individual declarations.

Perhaps that makes me a late bloomer, but I don't care. All that matters is that I'm here, eating food too complicated for me to make at home with a sauce that's so French, I can't pronounce it. Logan motions to his plate. "This was the moment I was going to tell you that I love you, for the record."

I snicker at his cuteness. "For the record, the way it came out was perfect. Besides, if we were declaring our love for the first time right now, then we couldn't be discussing the case, which has been eating at me all day long."

Logan's shoulders lower with a contented sigh. "As much as I don't like how much of my life my job takes over when something gets under my skin like this, I'm glad you're just as bothered by it. Then I don't drive myself crazy, going over it a hundred times all by my lonesome." He motions to me with his fork. "This way, I get to make us both nuts, talking about it and getting nowhere new."

I chuckle into my glass of water. "I have no idea what you're talking about. I certainly haven't been obsessing about the severed hand all day long, trying to figure out who could have possibly done something so horrible. I'm sure it also won't keep me up all night long until there's some sort of resolution."

When his head tilts to the side to take in the scope of my features, I can tell he is content. "I'm glad we found each other, and not just because I have no good theories on who might have done this. There's only the one I don't want to mention, because I hope I'm dead wrong. Got any theories on who it might be? Because I'm not ready to voice my guess."

"Well, I've got a theory, but not a good one. I'm in a similar boat, hoping my guess is wrong." I push my remaining spear of asparagus around on my plate, wishing I had a better guess as to who belongs behind bars.

"I'm all ears. You've been backing off that topic all evening. I can tell you don't want to pin the blame on anyone." He motions to himself. "I recognize the dance, because I'm doing it, too."

I keep my eyes on my food while I wait for the words to come. "I'm not sure he's guilty. I'm sure I'm reading it all wrong. But he was there, dropping off donations when I found the cookie jar. He was there before I found it, too, which means he could have been the one to add his donation to the top of the pile, which was where I started sorting when I got there." I scratch an itch on my nape. "And he told me that he'd been on a fishing trip with Rip and Bill last week, but when I asked Rip about it, he said they hadn't been in a while. That's..." I shrug, unsure how to brush off that tidbit. "That's probably normal." I gnaw on my lower lip. "It's also probably normal to have a hunting knife in one's glovebox that could most definitely saw through a wrist."

Logan's eyes are wide. "My suspect collects cookie jars. That's it. That's all I've got. You've got a knife, a false alibi and the person pegged at the scene of the crime? Tell me, Charlotte. How did you become better at being a cop than the guy with a badge?"

I snort at his compliment. "I'm not sure my clues will amount to anything. In fact, I sincerely hope they don't."

My boyfriend leans forward, the beautiful meal forgotten. "Who is it?"

"You first." I take a swallow of my water. "You tell me who the cookie jar collector is, so I'm not the only person falsely accusing someone." I lean my elbows on the table and massage my temples. "I really hope all I've got is a false accusation. If it's true, it'll break my heart."

Logan lowers his chin. "Okay, I'll go first." He pauses, taking a deep breath. "Betty collects cookie jars. I've been to her house and seen the shelf of cookie jars that stretches around the entire top of the kitchen." He shakes his head. "It sounds stupid even as I say it. As if owning a lot of cookie jars somehow makes you the suspect when a severed hand is found inside one at a completely different location than her house." He taps his heart. "Plus, I love Betty. She had the patience to try and teach me how to play the piano when I was young."

"You play the piano? I didn't know that."

Logan's neck shrinks. "No. Betty *tried* to teach me, but I'm admittedly a hopelessly non-musical person. I feel terrible for even suggesting her as the culprit. But Rip is her husband, who's been running the charity drive. If they wanted to offload a hand, where better to hide it than in plain sight, tousled in with the other donations?"

"It's not a hopeless theory," I grant him. "But Betty didn't do it. She's too wonderful." I wince. "Just like my suspect."

Logan sets down his fork. "You're killing me, Charlotte.

Who has a hunting knife on him, was at the donations area, and lied about where he was last week?"

I lower my head in shame. "It's Frank. But it can't be Frank. He's awesome. He's always been a friend to me. I adore Frank. I can't manage to wrap my mind around the fact that there are a handful of arrows pointing at him, telling me what can't be true—that Frank is guilty."

Logan is quiet while he gives my conscience time to sizzle in the air, instead of senselessly batting it away. "I'm sorry you've been carrying that around all day by yourself. Look, I want to know about your theories on the case because it's my job to investigate this, but I also know that it's eating you up inside to think negatively about someone you care for. Frank is a good guy. I'm sure you're right; it can't be him." He leans forward when my guilt is about to get the better of me. "So tomorrow morning, I'll do what I can to cross him off the list. Then you won't have to feel this anymore."

My spine lengthens when I realize that Logan hears me, and he's going to help. He's going to assume the best in Frank, even when the worst of it is pointed his way. "Thanks. And I can pop by Betty's sometime this week to pay my star employee a visit. Check out her cookie jar collection to see if anything fishy stands out. You know, to cross her off the suspect list, so you don't have to feel crummy anymore over someone you care about."

The corner of Logan's mouth lifts, revealing a dimple because he's just that handsome.

I breathe easier, knowing that he's got my back, and I've got his.

Just when I think things can't get any better, the waiter comes out with dessert, sealing Logan as the perfect man, and this as the perfect date.

7

BETTY'S COLLECTION

I didn't toss and turn all night, as I suspected I might with so many awful clues swimming around in my mind. The fact that Logan was going to make it his business to cross Frank off the list put part of my worries at ease, allowing me to sleep without brewing in frustration.

When I head down to the kitchen after my morning shower, Aunt Winnie pinches my cheek. Then she pours a mug with water after dropping in a teabag for me that matches the fragrance of hers. "Good morning, honey cake."

"Morning, favorite aunt."

She chortles as she gets out the honey, knowing I like my morning beverage sweeter than most. "Big day of baking ahead of you?"

I shake my head. "After my date last night, I went back

to the bakery and finished icing the cupcakes. I'm taking the morning off to help out at the charity drive after I run an errand."

"Rip is lucky to have you."

I let out a "pfft" sound. "He's lucky to have Marianne. She's like a general or something. She can look at a mess and know what needs to be done. She's incredible. I'm just along for the ride."

"Care to take in my box of donations? It'd save me a trip. After helping with the drive at the gymnasium, I realized that I have far more things than I know what to do with."

"Absolutely."

Aunt Winnie sits down at the kitchen table with me, and out comes the story of my date with Logan, and the business of us being in love and brave enough to say it aloud. It's a true treasure that my great-aunt cares about the details of my life. I don't have to hold back or downplay my excitement, afraid of sounding childish. She loves me, and that love frees me to be myself without apology.

"I can't believe how natural it all felt. How right."

Aunt Winnie smiles at me with the far-off look in her glassy sea-green eyes of a woman who knows exactly how wonderful it is to love and be loved. "Is it wrong that I want to pinch his cheeks because I'm so pleased about it all?"

I chuckle into my morning tea. "I'm sure he wouldn't mind that. He adores you."

"As he should." She stands slowly. "Speaking of

people we adore, I'm off to see Karen and Agnes this morning. We're going for a walk, then we're heading to the Cat's Pajamas to beg them to let us hold some puppies."

I sit up in my chair. "We're allowed to do that? I want to cuddle a puppy! Count me in next time you go."

"Already planned on it." She leans over and kisses the top of my head, further sealing in the feeling of cozy affection I never stop needing or appreciating. I love it here—in this house, in this town, in this happy, cuddly warmth that envelopes me on the days I crave it most.

After I finish my tea and toast, I load up my car with Aunt Winnie's donations and head over to run my errand of the morning. Sure, it's Betty's day off, and sure, she could probably use a break from seeing me, but as I pull into the driveway of Betty and Rip's address, I know that this is the only place I need to be. My perpetual employee of the month has saved my sanity on multiple occasions, so attention must be paid. If her anniversary is coming up, then I want to give her a smile that shines through her whole house.

The ranch-style home is neat as a pin on the outside, complete with an edged lawn and perfect petunias potted on the porch. Rip is so together; I'd expect nothing less.

I press the doorbell, holding a pink box with a slice of joy stored inside. I like making the world brighter with sugar.

But when Betty opens the door, her brow is furrowed,

and the phone is pressed to her cheek. "Oh! Hello, Charlotte. Come on in."

I shuffle inside while she sighs into the phone and then ends the call. I try not to let the knickknacks of cherub figurines littering the mantle distract my focus. I'm here to give Betty her anniversary gift, and also to scope her collection of cookie jars to see if anything is amiss. "Everything alright?"

Betty's usually cheery features are marred with concern as she sets her phone on the table beside the navy leather couch to give me a hug. Her track suit is neon pink today, making her round cheeks naturally rosy. "Probably. I think so. I hope so. Most likely."

Nothing about her reply is reassuring. My hip juts to the side as I fix my eyes on hers, taking in their concern. "Talk to me."

Betty shakes her head to dismiss her worry. "I'm sure it's fine. It's just that Delia was supposed to be home last night, and she's not. She's visiting her mother, and I promised to water her plants and take out her garbage. She got a pet turtle two weeks ago, and I'm supposed to be feeding him."

"I didn't know Delia got herself a pet turtle. How sweet!"

Betty nods. "Very sweet. His name is Michelangelo. I stop by to feed him and change his water in the morning. I wanted to make sure Delia got home alright so I could update her on Michelangelo, but she's not answering."

"I'm sure she's just sleeping in or something. Want me to drive by her house today? I can see if she's home and make sure the turtle is alright."

Betty squeezes my hand. "That's thoughtful of you, dear. No, no. I'll do it. If Delia's not there, I'll want to feed Michelangelo, so he doesn't get hungry if she's been delayed a few hours. It's just odd because Delia always picks up when I call." Her lips purse in concern. "I'm probably worrying over nothing. I'll call Frank if she's not there. Maybe he heard from her."

I return the affectionate squeeze, hoping it bolsters her a bit and soothes her nerves. "I'm sure she just decided to take an extra day on her vacation and forgot to mention it."

Betty nods, but she doesn't look the least bit convinced that her worry is unfounded, which isn't something I can confidently speak to. "Probably." She takes in my presence in her home with new eyes. "To what do I owe the pleasure of this visit, Charlotte? You come over to say hello, and I'm scattering my worry all over the place."

The pink box in my hands makes its way to hers. "I chose a flavor of the month, and I thought you might like the first taste, since you inspired it."

Betty's smile spreads across her face. "How did I manage to do that?"

"It's your anniversary coming up. I thought you and Rip could use a trip down memory lane and have a taste of the dessert you shared on your honeymoon."

Betty's mouth falls open when she flips up the lid of the small pink box with my logo on the top. "Is this..."

Happiness sweeps through me while I take in the wonder that I was hoping she would experience. "Forty-nine years deserves a celebration with something sweet. It's a key lime cupcake with a key lime whipped cream frosting. Graham cracker crumbles on top."

Betty takes out the cupcake and peels off the wrapper, not bothering to wait for her husband, who is hard at work at the charity drive already, even though it is barely nine in the morning. I watch Betty take her first bite, which is my favorite part of the entire baking process. The closing of the eyes, the "mm" noise, the inhale followed by the contented exhale.

Every. Single. Time.

Never gets old.

Betty doesn't say a word but goes in for a second bite and a third, not stopping until the entire cupcake is a litter of crumbs in the wrapper, which she swipes up with her sticky finger. "Oh, Charlotte. This is a winner. You really did this for me?"

I nod, grateful that the people I adore understand me enough to know that this is how I express my appreciation for the special ones in my life.

Betty sets the pink box with the remaining cupcake down and wraps me in a hug that feels like a blanket cuddled around my very soul. I don't know how I lived for so many years without friends who hug as easily as breathing, but I know for certain that I came alive when I stepped into the sunshine of Sweetwater Falls, and the love that resides here.

"Thank you, boss."

I chuckle at the title. "Anything for my employee of the month."

When she pulls back, she invites me into the kitchen, where I remember the less jolly reason why I am here. "Oh, wow! Betty, I've never seen so many cookie jars in one place." And it's true. The shelf that stretches along the top foot of the kitchen has been painted a forest green to match the curtains over the window near the sink. The dark color naturally draws the eye up, revealing a collection of cookie jars that is as unique as it is precious.

"It's my little obsession. I switched to collecting cherub figurines a few years ago when I ran out of shelf space. I know it's silly, but I love cookie jars."

"I love cookies, so I can't complain about your collection. So cool! Is that one from the *Wizard of Oz*?"

"Sure is. You've never appreciated chocolate chip cookies more than when they come out of ruby slippers."

"The details on some of these. So intricate!" Each cookie jar has a story to tell, and personality to broadcast. They aren't just round vases with lids; they're something that would make a naturally jolly woman grin when she used them.

Betty nods. I can tell she likes that I am enthralled by her eclectic taste. "Oh, yes. I don't bother with the boring ones. It has to be fun. It has to be something that I specifically love. Cookie jars aren't anything special normally, so when I see one I fall in love with, I bring it home."

I mull over her words, fitting them into the profile of a truly innocent person whom Logan can safely cross off his list of suspects. "So, it's not just any cookie jar. It needs to be a fun one that means something to you."

Betty motions to one that looks like a treehouse, complete with fairies perched on the branches. "Absolutely. The jar has to be more exciting than the cookies inside, which is a tall order, because I make truly fantastic chocolate chip cookies."

My shoulders relax as I smile at her. "I have no doubt. You don't have any normal cookie jars. I'd expect nothing less than absolute personality coming from you. I'm glad your collection is a true reflection of you."

Betty gazes at the jars appreciatively. "Thank you, dear."

Just to make sure, I try to mentally stack another cookie jar on the shelf, recalling the very plain design of the thing that surely would not appeal to Betty, nor would it be something she would add to her collection. It was a brown, drab thing with "Cookies" scripted on the side. The vessel was without a stitch of decoration or personality to it before I broke the thing and revealed the gore inside.

There's no way that could fit on the shelf up here; it's packed tight without room for a single additional jar. Just to be sure, I ask her, "This shelf is full, alright. Do you have extra cookie jars around the house or in storage?"

Betty shakes her head. "No. Once the shelf was filled, I pulled back and switched to cherub figurines. But I like the idea of putting a few around the house. Who wouldn't want a fun cookie jar by their bedside? Maybe I'll try that." She feathers her fingers together, and I can tell she is already envisioning the perfect spot to place her next great find. "You're evil, opening my mind to bring more cookie jars into the house. I thought I was finished, but if one more comes my way that I just have to have, I know exactly where I can put it."

I love the look of intrigue mingled with joy on Betty's face. She deserves every good thing. So much the better if that thing is filled with cookies.

After I leave, I call Logan on my way to the charity drive. "It's not Betty," I inform him. "She doesn't have a spot left open where a missing cookie jar might've been, and the one that I broke at the charity drive was plain, which isn't the kind of cookie jar Betty collects. She only likes the fancy kinds, and she doesn't have a stock of them squirreled away in storage. What you see is what you get."

Logan's sigh is equal parts relief and frustration. "I suppose that's a good thing. I don't want Betty to have been guilty. However, that means I've only got Frank as a suspect, and he's looking guiltier by the hour."

"How so?" I turn onto the main thoroughfare, my car creeping forward at the standard thirty-five miles per hour that runs through the entire small town.

"He's not here."

I frown as I come to a stop sign. "What do you mean?"

"I mean the Nosy Newsy is closed, and he isn't at his house."

My top two front teeth worry my lower lip, unsure if this is a crisis or just a nothing of a coincidence. "It's normal for a person to take a day off. Maybe he decided to go fishing." Another thought pops into my head. "Delia was supposed to be back from her trip to her mother's last night, but Betty mentioned she hasn't been back yet. Maybe she's on a breakfast date with Frank."

I can tell Logan is talking himself down from jumping to conclusions, as well. "Sure. But now you're telling me that Delia is missing? Delia is missing, and her boyfriend is suspected of murder?"

I wince. "I'm sure that's not what I meant to have said. She's not officially missing. She's just a little late coming back from out of town. That's normal. Delia probably decided to stay another night at her mother's and didn't feel the need to tell the entire town about it."

It's clear to me that Logan is not convinced that worry is unnecessary. "Perhaps. But I'm going to reach out to Delia myself to see if I can nail down her location. At least get confirmation that she hasn't been murdered."

I was hoping to be peppy and productive for the

charity drive, so I could be Marianne's number one helper. But by the time I pull into the high school gymnasium's parking lot, I am certain that every conversation will be partially clouded with thoughts of Delia while I cross my fingers for her safety.

8

NEW SYSTEM

*M*arianne is a wonder to behold. While I always admire my best friend, watching her cast aside her meek personality to take charge of chaos is a thing of beauty. "Over to the home goods section with that," she says to Sally, pointing to the left side of the gymnasium.

"What happened to the mountain of clothing?" I ask her. "I was planning on hiding out inside of it later. I thought it might make a comfy place to take a nap."

Marianne keeps her eyes on her task while she speaks. "I'm sure the mountain will be back in an hour or two. People seem to want to purge their closets this year." She motions to a spot beside her purse next to the bleachers. "I've already found two sweaters that I'm going to buy. Gotta pace myself, though. I don't want to fill all the space I just gained in my closet after I got rid of the clothes I don't want anymore."

"Good thinking. You want this over here?" I ask of a tall lamp, which could go in furniture but could also be considered home goods.

Marianne nods. "Yes, I..." But when her gaze drifts to the entrance, her mouth firms with displeasure. "Unbelievable."

I follow her eyeline, seeing Kurt, Dwight's father, in the doorway, twisting his fingers anxiously. "What's wrong? Is Kurt not supposed to be here?"

"His second time this morning. I don't know why people think they can donate things and then expect for us to wade through the sorted piles to give them back their stuff. When you donate it, it stays here. For all I care, he can buy it back when the sale happens."

It's an uncharacteristically tart response from Marianne, which begs me to give her a closer look. Her pixie cut isn't as buoyant today. Her usual smile is gone, and there are bags under her eyes. "Everything okay, Marianne?" I ask quietly while the other volunteers migrate around the place, each doing their assigned tasks.

Marianne's shoulders sag as she exhales her stress, leaning her fists on the nearest table. "I don't know."

I've been here for five whole minutes, and I didn't notice until just now that she's having a crisis that she's been carrying around by herself. I take hold of her wrist and lead her away from the bustle of movement to the back of the gymnasium, where no one can overhear. "What's going on?"

She pinches the bridge of her nose. "Nothing. Everything. I don't know. I'm too in my head about it, which I'm sure is just making it worse."

"Making what worse? What happened?"

Marianne presses her lips together, and I can tell she is debating waving me off with a dismissive "nothing" and calling it a day. But when I cross my arms over my chest, keeping compassion firm on my face, I make it clear that she is going to talk about whatever it is that's bothering her.

No wonder she's been so dedicated to the charity drive. She's using the endless work to avoid whatever problem has been plaguing her.

"It's Carlos. We had an argument last night, and we haven't spoken since."

Granted, that's not a whole lot of time passed, but I don't think it would be helpful to point that out. "What was the fight about?"

Marianne smooths a piece of brown hair back from her face, showing off more of her pretty olive skin. "I don't even know how it happened. We were talking about my house, and I mentioned that it was the perfect place for me. He said that one-bedroom homes are fine, but that he needs a dedicated office for him to be able to live somewhere. I told him that he doesn't have to put my house down, just because it's not big enough for his liking. He doesn't live there. What does he care? I felt like he was calling me poor, or saying my house wasn't impressive enough. I like where I live. It was callous, and we ended the call with frustration still lingering between us. Not good."

"Very not good."

"I still can't believe he would say that."

I try to hide my smirk, but it's a bad job because her eyes widen with indignation at my seeming amusement at her plight. "I'm sorry!" I offer, but my smile only broadens more.

"What's so funny?" Her nose crinkles, and she looks as if she is gearing up for her second argument in as many days.

"What's funny is that Carlos wasn't criticizing your house. Not really. He was hinting at wanting a future with you. He was trying to dance around telling you that when you two do live together someday, he isn't sure if it can be at your house, because he needs an office wherever he lives."

Marianne's face pulls as if she'd very much like to tell me I'm way off base. Her mouth opens and then slams shut. Then her eyes widen as her jaw drops. "Oh!"

I chuckle, accidentally snorting my amusement at the misunderstanding that has probably left poor Carlos thinking Marianne has never even considered the possibility of more with him. "Think I might be right?"

Marianne's entire body lifts as she clasps her hands under her chin. "Oh, Charlotte! Do you really think so?"

"I really do. Maybe you should call Carlos and tell him you're on the same page."

Marianne nods, but then hesitates. "I shouldn't take a break. Whenever I'm away for even five minutes, the system falls to chaos."

I wave her off toward the hallway. "Go. I'll do what I can to hold down the fort in your absence. Talk to Carlos. Make up and tell him how badly you want a future with him. Tell your boyfriend he's the handsomest lawyer you've ever met."

Marianne beams at me. "Thanks, Charlotte." She pauses and stares at her hands as if she can't believe the turn her life has taken in the course of a conversation. "Is this real?"

I bump my hip to hers, my smile bright because I love it when something good happens for my best friend. "Absolutely."

Marianne grabs up her phone and moves into the hallway so she can set things right with Carlos, leaving me to pretend I know how to work her system of organization. I press my lips together, focusing on the one person who seems to need immediate attention. "Hi, Kurt," I say to Dwight's father. "You look concerned. Anything I can help you with?"

The wiry, balding man wrings his hands, his nerves on clear display for the public. That, or his Parkinson's is giving him issue, and he's trying to cover the jerky involuntary movements with purposeful hand wringing. "I was telling that person over there that I donated something by mistake. I need to be able to get it back. If someone else took it home?" He shakes his head. "I'd never forgive myself."

I have no idea what the policy for something like that is, so I opt for kindness, since that is the town in which we live. "Sure thing. That sounds stressful. I can help you look for it. What is it?"

Kurt's eyes widen and he shakes his head as if he's been caught mid-criminal act. "No! No, I can find it. I mean, thank you. The librarian offered to help me find it, too, but I need to look for myself. It's..." he pauses, leaning in to whisper to me, "It's private."

I nod, unsure what could possibly have been donated that I can't know about. "No problem. Do me a favor and don't mess up the piles too badly? We're trying to keep things organized, and it's an uphill battle at this point."

Kurt exhales with relief and throws his arms around me, surprising a squeak from my lungs. "Thank you! I've been up all night looking for it, and I'm driving myself crazy. Thank you. I won't mess anything up. I'll find it and get out."

"Not a problem, Kurt." Motioning to the left, I explain to him the broad scope of the layout, so he can narrow down his search. "That section is clothing." Then I extend my arm to the right. "That's things, and ahead of us is furniture. I hope that helps. And again, if I can help you, let me know. Happy to keep an eye out, and I'm sure the other volunteers wouldn't mind, either."

"No, no. I've got it. Thank you. I'll be out of your hair faster than you can say, 'Hey, Kurt! Get out of my hair!'"

We share a giggle before I leave him to his needle in a haystack search. For the next half hour, donations keep coming in. After a failed attempt at trying to sort the boxes once they are dropped off, I decide life is too short to constantly be behind the eight-ball. I station a harried volunteer at the door, so he can take a break from sorting and greet the donors before they drop anything off.

"Can we really do that?" Hunter asks me, a guilty smile on his features as we leave his boyfriend to man the door.

I shrug at my friend. Hunter is about two inches shorter than me, but his moussed light-blond hair makes up the difference of my five-foot-ten height. "Dunno, but it's happening. People can sort their own things. I've got a volunteer at each station, and they'll make sure only those things are put on their tables. If this doesn't work, we'll go back to the way we were doing things before." I bump my elbow to his and point to the hill—not mountain—in the center of the gymnasium. "Now you and I can sort through the remaining donations without things constantly being added to the pile, if your boyfriend can catch people at the door and explain the system."

Hunter slaps his hands together, a winded smile on his face. "I like the sound of that, Charlie. Todd has been looking for a way to meet more people in town, anyway. Good thinking to have him at the door. I'll take the home goods, seeing as how they weren't so kind to you earlier this week."

I grimace. "You heard about that?"

Hunter nods. "I came in to volunteer as the cops were leaving. Yikes. You alright after finding a severed appendage like that?"

I hold my hand parallel to the floor and tilt it from side to side. "I'm definitely looking forward to the day when I don't recall what it was like, seeing a woman's severed hand tumble out of a smashed cookie jar."

Hunter winces. "Sick."

Though, he's younger than I am, so I can't tell if he's commenting on how cool that experience was for me, or if he legitimately agrees that whoever did such a thing was sick in the head.

We work in tandem, just as we did when I filled in for Gus at the Soup Alleyoop—a basketball-themed soup restaurant. It's nice to be able to dig into a project with both hands, pushing aside the niggling thoughts in my mind that taunt me about not having solved the mystery.

When Marianne emerges, she balks at the hill of donations that is now half the size it was when she left it. "What happened? I thought I would come back, and it would be madness."

I beam at her, straightening proudly with a stack of sweaters hanging off my arms. "We've got a doorman now," I say, motioning to Hunter's boyfriend. "And people aren't dropping off their donations anymore; they're sorting them with the help of the volunteers who are stationed at each category. It's not foolproof, but hey, look at how tiny Mount Donations is now."

Marianne's eyes are wide as she commemorates our effort with applause. "I love it. I can't believe how calm it is in here now. I don't want to pull my hair out in here when it's like this."

Of course, that is the exact moment when we hear raised voices from the doorway. "I just need to look!"

I roll my eyes and hold up my hand to Marianne, who puffs her chest as if readying to referee a professional wrestling match. "I got this. Kurt was just in here, looking for something he accidentally donated. It didn't take him more than fifteen minutes to either find it or not find it. No biggie."

Marianne's shoulders deflate. "Well, I guess I'll help with the donation pile, then."

I give her an encouraging smile and then head over to the front door, where a woman I don't recognize is talking animatedly with her hands, her pitch raised in a show of anxiety. "Please! I won't take anything I didn't donate."

I bump Todd's fist with mine. "Hey, Todd. I'll take it from here. You can explain the system to the next person in line." A friendly smile seems to dissipate a portion of the woman's angst as she turns her focus to me. "Hi, I'm Charlotte McKay. I don't think we've met."

"Janet. Janet Pilsner. I'm so sorry, but I need to get my

box of donations back. I donated something that belongs to my husband, and he's tearing out his hair about it. I'm so sorry!"

Janet has dull, brown hair in need of washing, and worry rounding her umber eyes. She looks to be around twenty-five years old, saddled with the worries of someone with too much on their plate.

Fixing her with my best understanding expression, I wind my arm through hers and bring her into the gymnasium. "It happens. Sounds like a frustrating morning for you."

"It really has been. I'm so sorry I'm bothering you with this. I didn't think Charles wanted that old sweater! But apparently, it's super important to him, even though he's never worn it before, and it's three sizes too small." She casts me a conspiratorial look as she rolls her eyes. "Men, am I right?"

I truly can't speak to that. I can't imagine Logan making me feel bad because I donated something he doesn't use. Then again, I probably wouldn't donate something of his without his knowledge.

Then again, dating is different than being married, so I'm not sure what I would do in a situation I've never been in. Either way, I know that the person I am today understands how to empathize, so I lead Janet to the men's clothing section, which thankfully, is starting to become far more organized, now that the clothing volunteers can breathe a little. I give Janet's shoulder a squeeze before I explain her situation to the volunteer, giving her permission to leaf through the clothing while warning her gently not to make a huge mess of things.

I wish her well and return to the donation pile as a queue of donors at the door begins to build up while Todd explains the system in great detail.

"Janet alright?" Marianne asks me.

I leaf through the pile, searching for enough women's clothing to fill my arms. "I think so. A little worked up."

Marianne nods contemplatively. "She only gets worked up about Charles, her husband. I've never seen a man throw as many fits as he does. She wasn't always afraid of her own shadow, apologizing for everything, whether it needs it or not."

My lips purse while I mull over the implications of what Marianne is saying. "Well, I hope she finds his sweater."

Marianne murmurs a quiet, "I hope she finds a divorce attorney."

I grimace, taking in Janet with new light as she sifts through the clothing with frantic fingers, hoping to make peace with a man who might never be satisfied with her best efforts.

9

WORRY TORNADO

One of the perks of running a cupcakery in a friendly small town is that every Friday morning from nine until noon, I get to hand out the orders. I greet my customers by name as they pick up their boxes of cupcakes one by one. I never interacted with people this often when I lived in a big city, and I'm sure if I totaled up the number of people in my entire life who knew my name before I moved here, the small town of Sweetwater Falls would still prove to be a higher number. They care about the personal touches here. They like to stand around and chat when the weather is nice after they've retrieved their order.

Marcus McManus is one of my favorite people, mostly because he brings his dog Rigby along, which gives me a chance to play with the beautiful golden retriever. "Thanks, Charlotte. I'm hosting my movie night this weekend. Ever since you opened your shop, I never have to think about what I'm going to put out for my friends. Easy-peasy."

I grin at him as I kneel to pet his dog. I love the soft fur, and the gentle eyes that regard me as though I'm someone special. "What's the movie this time?"

"*Jaws*," he says to me. "I figure that's a good summertime movie. A little cupcake. A little shark attack. It's a recipe for a good movie night. Plus, unlimited popcorn. The only problem is I might get carried away and quote the thing line by line." Then Marcus starts doing exactly that, his short brown hair staying in place while his tall frame moves with what I am assuming is great accuracy to mimic his favorite parts.

I kiss Rigby's furry cheek after grinning at Marcus' antics. "Never seen it, but I'm sure that's a spot-on impersonation."

Marcus' jaw drops as he ceases all movement. "I hope that's a sick joke."

I snicker at what he considers a serious breach of happiness. "Never had the stomach for scary movies."

Marcus takes several steps back, holding his hand over his heart as if I've shot him with my callous words. "No. No, no. You can't be serious. And if you are, I cannot continue to let this go on. What are you doing tomorrow night?" Before I can answer, he chimes in with a reply. "I'll tell you what you're doing. You'll be coming over to my place to watch *Jaws*. If you don't agree, I'll stand right here and act it out, scene by scene for the next ninety minutes."

I chuckle into his dog's yellow-beige fur. "Anything but that! I'm not sure I can make it tomorrow night, and I know I can't handle a scary movie about sharks if I ever want to set foot in the water again. Maybe another movie night, though. Does Lisa like scary movies?"

He beams at the mention of his girlfriend. "She sure does. Pretends she's all scared sometimes so we can cuddle close. She has a yoga class that runs late tomorrow, but she said she'll be there by the time the movie starts. Bring Logan along whenever you can make it to my movie nights on the weeks the flick isn't too scary for you. I haven't had the chance to hang out with him in a long time."

"I'll see what I can do." I wave goodbye to them, then hand out the next several boxes of cupcakes, grateful when the orders are half gone by the time Betty comes in for her shift. It's technically not her shift, but she loves handing out cupcakes to people. Just like me, she looks forward to greeting the townsfolk who make her come alive.

Plus, when she's managing the door, I can do fancy things like clean my kitchen. Every Friday morning, it looks like a chocolate bomb went off in my commercial kitchen, and every Friday morning, I am grateful that Betty is here, so I can get the space back to zero. It takes a lot of elbow grease and a few hours of focus to clean everything so there isn't any grime building up in the hard-to-reach places. I like my quiet cleaning time, mostly because I can be productive while my mind unwinds itself from everything in my week that I haven't made peace with yet.

Mainly, my mind drifts to the severed hand, which as it turns out, isn't something one can scrub from their memory quickly or easily. As I wipe away the flour and sugar that have made it into far corners and under shelves, I try my best at visualizing wiping my worries away.

It doesn't seem to be working.

When there are only a dozen orders left and zero cars in the parking lot, Betty comes back inside with a frown, which is unlike her.

"What's wrong, Betty?"

She waves off my concern, but her white-blonde brow is knit, and her mouth drawn in a tight line. "I'm in a worry tornado, I'm afraid."

I take a breather from scrubbing the floors that stretch under the counters and sit back on my butt on the floor. "Any sign of the worry weather breaking?"

Betty shakes her head. "None on the horizon." She motions to the boxes on the counter. "I was hoping Delia would be back to pick up her order."

"Delia ordered cupcakes?" I crane my neck, but I can't see the tops of the boxes from here. "I didn't look at who placed orders for this week." Betty's handwriting is prettier than mine, so she takes it upon herself to label the names on the boxes in her seamless calligraphy.

Betty taps a box on the end. "I got all excited when I saw that she'd ordered a box of cupcakes. She hasn't been answering her phone, and from what I can tell, she hasn't been back from her trip out of town. I don't mind feeding her turtle, but she should have been back by now. I'm getting worried something's happened to her. I've never gone this long without hearing from Delia."

I wipe the sweat from my forehead. "Have you tried talking to Frank?"

Betty wipes her palms off on her bright yellow track suit. "I thought I'd do exactly that this morning, but he's got Dwight working the Nosy Newsy. Kurt told me Frank had to take the weekend off."

"Maybe Frank and Delia decided to take a long weekend together."

"Maybe, but you'd think Delia would have asked me to keep looking after her turtle. And if that's true, then why isn't she able to answer my calls? I'm telling you; something doesn't feel right about this."

I don't want to add to her growing concern by telling her that something has felt off to me from the beginning of this, as well. I gaze up at Betty, pushing my strawberry blonde tangles from my face so I can take in the scope of my friend's upset. "Hey, I'm sure everything is okay. There's a logical explanation for it all." I try not to validate the concern that both of us are feeling. "Any chance you know her mother's address? If it's not too far, I can go check on her."

Betty shakes her head. "It's several hours away. And I'm not officially worried."

"Want me to feed her turtle this afternoon?"

Betty shoots me a look of gratitude. "I'd actually really appreciate it. Rip and I have plans. We're supposed to go on a date for our anniversary. We won't have much alone time once the charity drive starts on Thursday."

"Go and have the best time. I'll feed the turtle. I'm nearly finished here, anyway."

"Thank you, dear. Instructions are beside the tank. Key is under the ceramic turtle on the porch."

I stand and wrap my sweaty arms around my friend. "Oh, Betty. I'm sure Delia is alright." But as I say the words, I hear the falsity ringing in them. We both know that I'm not sure of that at all. But I want it to be true, so for the moment, I hope it is.

10

MYSTERIOUS MAIL

*A*gnes is the last person who comes to pick up her box of cupcakes. She enjoys being the last one, because then we can stand around and chat for however long she likes. I miss her face. I feel as if I've been far too busy with work and the charity drive, and I haven't had the chance to catch up with one of the most important people in my life.

"You're *what*?"

Agnes acts as if she hasn't said anything strange in the slightest. "I'm going to go play disc golf in the park with the girls. Of course, I have no idea how to play, but the Miller boys are going to teach us."

I pinch the bridge of my nose after I finish washing my hands in the sink. "Let me get this straight. You're going to the park with Aunt Winnie and Karen and the rowdy

Miller boys, and you're all going to play disc golf, which you don't know how to play?"

Agnes bobs her head confidently, as if nothing strange is happening in the slightest. "That's the size of it. I saw Laura about ready to pull her hair out yesterday. I'm not brave enough to take on all three Miller boys by myself, but I figure if each member of the Live Forever Club takes a child, we'll most likely survive."

"Love the confidence. You might want Marianne to be standing by. She's the only one I've ever seen who can handle those boys." I had to bring her in when I foolishly had a similar heartbreak for Laura Miller's plight and volunteered to babysit. If I hadn't had Marianne and Carlos come in to help me, I might have been the one tearing out my hair. As it was, we survived the night, but it was only because we divided and conquered, each of us taking one Miller boy under our wing.

Agnes taps her rounded chin. "Not a bad idea. But I think Marianne is working today at the library. I thought perhaps we could take the boys to there to pick out a few books after our round of disc golf. Marianne might come in handy then."

I cannot fathom the trio of Miller boys in a library, where the atmosphere is supposed to be filled with learning and quiet.

I hug Agnes after a few more minutes of chatting, and then take the lone pink box that never got picked up. Delia's name in Betty's impressive calligraphy speaks to me like an omen of doom. The noon deadline of picking up cupcake orders has come and gone, and still there is no sign of Delia. I shoot her a text that I'll be feeding her turtle today, and then head over to her house in my red sedan. Sure enough, on my way to her house, I see that the Nosy Newsy stand is being managed by Dwight, who is wearing a mascot costume to make himself look like a giant slice of watermelon. I'm not completely sure what a watermelon slice has to do with newspapers, but he looks happy, and there seem to be plenty of people milling around, so I guess the residents of Sweetwater Falls prefer their daily news with a side of watermelon today.

When I arrive at Delia's home, I empty the mailbox and bring the mailers into the house, greeting her turtle, whose name I can't remember. It was one of the ninja turtles. I recall that much. "Hey there, little buddy. Everything okay?" I set Delia's cupcake box on the counter beside the growing pile of mail.

I locate the container of turtle pellets, read the back of the bottle and shake the proper amount into the aquarium. Then I empty the water container and refill it with fresh water.

I tap on the glass, but the turtle doesn't seem to care if anyone is here for him to talk to or not. "I thought you might be lonely, being here for so long by yourself. Any ideas what might have happened to your mother?"

The turtle doesn't answer, which is a bummer.

Instead of having a one-way conversation with a turtle,

I decide to leave Delia a note. I mosey to her kitchen and pull open a drawer at random, guessing that at some point, I will find myself a junk drawer with a paper and pen. By the fourth one, I find what I need and slap the pad of paper on the counter. My movements are ungraceful, and I accidentally knock the pile of mail onto the floor.

The turtle catches sight of my grimace, but thankfully, doesn't laugh at my clumsiness. I kneel on the linoleum and scoop up armloads of mailers, newspapers, and other pieces of mail. I can't just leave them haphazardly on the counter, so I sort the mail, making a pile for the newspapers, then another for what I'm pretty sure is junk mail, and then the rest for bills.

That is, until I see something that looks personal. It's got Delia's name handwritten on the envelope in a slanted scribble, with no address anywhere. I frown at the sealed envelope as I speak my confusion aloud to the turtle. "Someone came by the house and dropped a letter in Delia's mailbox? That's odd."

Curiosity burns in me, so I know I have to get out of here before I do something crazy and open the letter. I text Betty, sending her a picture of the envelope and asking her if she has any idea who it might be from.

Betty calls me back seconds after the text goes through. "No idea. And I didn't take in that piece of mail. I would have noticed if someone sent her something without an address on the envelope."

"It's probably nothing. I mean, this isn't a big deal,

right?"

"Is it sealed?"

"Sure is. But that's fine. People do that, right? Leave letters in people's mailboxes instead of mailing them. It doesn't have anything to do with Delia going missing."

Betty's voice sounds firm. "Open it, and let's find out."

I hiss at the crime I am unwilling to commit. "Betty! I would never do something so illegal. This is her personal mail. This letter belongs to Delia."

"Charlotte, if Delia goes missing, and she's also getting mysterious letters sent to her home, that's got to mean something. Open the letter, and let's find out."

"I'm about to give you a proper reprimand, young lady." I do my best to make my voice as stern as possible. "I shouldn't have texted you anything. Go back to your date and have a good time. I'm sure Delia is on her way home as we speak."

Betty clucks her tongue at me. "What would Winifred say?"

I sigh. "She would scold me for being a rule follower, but that doesn't change the fact that that is exactly what I am."

"Remind me to explain to your aunt that she needs to teach you how to steam a letter open. Then no one will know what you've done, and we'll for sure know that Delia is or is not being stalked by someone putting something in her mailbox."

After we end the call, I gnaw on my lower lip, contemplating the very real temptation to go off-book and do something I know is wrong. Delia has a right to privacy. She's got a right to open her own mail without me sticking my nose in the middle of it. I know I should put down the envelope and leave right now.

I shouldn't turn on the kettle atop the stove.

I shouldn't turn the envelope over in my hands, waiting for the water to boil and the steam to undo the adhesive that has the envelope glued shut.

I know what I *shouldn't* do.

My eyes widen as I realize I am on the verge of breaking a law on a whim. I shut off the stove, place the envelope on the counter with the rest of the mail, and run out of Delia's house before I find myself unable to resist the temptation.

I shouldn't have let myself go through her mail. As I grip the steering wheel after buckling myself into the car, all I can think is that perhaps Delia is in real danger, and I am too chicken to take a look at the clue that was staring me in the face.

I sit in the driveway for several minutes, daring myself to go in while lecturing myself to stay out. It's not until I hear the soprano honk of a golf cart behind me that I realize Betty wasn't bluffing about telling my great-aunt.

I lean my forehead to my steering wheel when it becomes clear that the Live Forever Club isn't about to let me off the hook. They will always be there to push me toward a life that I may not be ready to seize.

11

EAVESDROPPERS

The afternoon is filled with sunshine and the fragrant scent of a rosebush coming from across the street. If not for the pressure bearing down on me, I would be perfectly content. I grimace when my Aunt Winnie raps her knuckles on my car window. "I hear we have a giant chicken inside this very car."

I sink down in my seat and cover my face with my hands. "A giant chicken posing as a rule follower."

Aunt Winnie shakes her head at me as she clucks her tongue. "The worst kind. Let's go, honey cake."

I unbuckle and head back into the house behind my great-aunt, wondering when it was that I let the rules get in the way of the goal. If I want to make sure Delia is okay, then perhaps checking that she's not being sent unmarked threatening notes is a good place to start.

But it's also illegal.

Aunt Winnie turns on the kettle and sifts through the mail until she finds the infamous letter. "Your timing couldn't have been more perfect. The Miller boys are set on tearing apart the park, blade of grass by blade of grass. If Karen and Agnes ask, you were having an emergency and desperately needed my help—which isn't too far off the mark."

"I don't... We shouldn't..."

"Oh, but we should, and we are. If Delia's in real trouble, she's not going to mind us opening her mail. And if she's not, then let this be a lesson to her that she shouldn't disappear on us, or we're going to do all we can to make sure she's okay." Aunt Winnie holds the envelope aloft, waiting for the steam to unlock the secrets inside.

Biting on my nails, I try to keep my nerves at bay while we let the silence fill Delia's home.

Aunt Winnie motions to a baby monitor on the kitchen counter. "Is Delia expecting? Because I can't imagine why else she would have a baby monitor in her home."

I grimace because I've seen that thing in use before. "Um, not that I know of. She keeps that on during the day because the neighbors across the street are usually arguing, and Delia likes to listen in. She calls it her favorite show." Just saying it aloud makes me feel gross.

Aunt Winnie considers the object before turning it on and letting a semi-familiar female voice fill the house. "I don't know why you're still upset. I found your sweater that

I donated by mistake. It's right here, and you're still not wearing it because it's still too small for you."

"That's Janet," I tell Aunt Winnie.

Winnie chortles at Delia's deviance. "My goodness. No wonder Delia always has the latest gossip. She's listening in on people's private conversations inside their homes!" Aunt Winnie musses my hair with her free hand. "And you were upset about opening her mail."

"I'm still upset about it! But I'm coming around to your side. I know it's wrong, but if Delia is hurt, I need all the information, so we can help her if she needs it."

A man's voice filters through the air. "I'm mad because you went through my things without asking! I should be able to have a little privacy, you know. What else did you take? Because I can't get up into the attic to check to make sure all my stuff is still there. The space is too narrow. Man! First my mother is a pain, and now you! It's like I'm surrounded by idiots!"

Janet doesn't sound sure of anything. "I... I don't think I packed anything else that was yours. That was all! I can't reach much up there, either. I just grabbed that first box. It was all I could reach."

"Don't go looking through my stuff! Are you stupid? How would you like it if I went flipping through your diary?" I can hear a baby crying behind Charles' shouting.

"You did that last week!" Janet replies in a hushed tone. "There, there, Rachel. It's okay."

"And you didn't like when I read your diary, did you?"

I turn off the baby monitor, my stomach churning after just a few seconds of Charles' wrath. "I can't listen any longer."

Aunt Winnie's upper lip curls. She rarely wears a look of complete disdain, but she aims it in Charles' direction to the house across the street. "I think Charles is going to start doing some listening to me if he doesn't learn how to speak to his wife with a little respect."

I don't know much about marriage, only that two people who care about each other should at least try to be kind, especially when there's a baby in the room who can be very much affected by the sound of yelling. I didn't have the courage to open Delia's letter, but before I can talk myself out of it, I locate the bravery to walk out the door and march across the street, ringing the doorbell to interrupt the fight. I can't solve their quarrel, but I can at least get Janet some fresh air.

I can hear Charles yelling through the closed door, but when the doorbell chimes through their home, his voice quiets.

Janet opens the door with moisture dotting her lashes and her baby in her arms. "Oh! Charlotte?"

I beam at her, as if nothing has ever been wrong in the world. "Hi, Janet. I was in the area, and Delia told me you live here." I work quickly to pull a lie out of my back pocket. "I was thinking of buying a house on this street. Feel like taking me for a walk to show me around?"

Janet barely takes in my obvious fib before agreeing.

"Absolutely. Let me grab the stroller." The door shuts, and their voices are far more hushed this time before she comes out with her baby in the stroller.

I watch her maneuver the thing down the one-step porch with ease, though I cannot imagine how I would attempt such a feat. "Your baby is adorable. What's her name?"

"This is Rachel."

"Well, she's lovely. Hi, Rachel." I wave at the baby. I don't have much experience being around babies, but I figure that passes as a proper greeting.

"Your timing couldn't have been better, Charlotte. I needed some fresh air."

"I can understand that. Full disclosure: I'm not really looking to buy a house in the area. I was feeding Delia's turtle, and I overheard a bit of yelling. Thought you could use a breather."

Janet and I start down the sidewalk with her chin lowered. "You heard that?"

"I'm sorry. Sounds like you're having a hard day."

Janet nods, her brown hair falling forward to obscure part of her face. "I can't seem to do anything right. Charles was upset when he tripped over one of Rachel's toys, so I thought I would clean up the house and donate a bunch of stuff we weren't using. Turns out, I donated the wrong things. He's upset. I should have asked if he wanted to keep that sweater. He's trying to get up into the attic to put the sweater back up there, but it's hard to get in there, so he's mad about that." Her hands grip the stroller's bar so hard that her knuckles turn white. "I didn't mean to make such a mess of things."

I don't know Janet. I don't know how she met Charles, or even how old her baby is. I don't know what she needs or how to say the perfect thing. So, instead of trying to insert myself into her choices when her life is her own and not mine, I reach out and trill my fingernails up and down her back to soothe a portion of her angst. "I'm sorry things are so hard."

I'm not sure if that was the right thing to say or the very wrong thing. Either way, Janet's eyes fill with fresh tears that start trailing down her cheeks. "Maybe tomorrow will be better." Though, the way she says it sounds like she's tried to cheer herself up with this many times before, and the tune is starting to ring off-key.

"I think it will be," I say to her with a touch more conviction. "Because tomorrow, you're going to bring Rachel over, and we're going to do something fun together."

Janet's head snaps up at me, her watery umber eyes brimming with a mix of wonder and questions. "We are?"

I nod, as if I've got any clue as to how to entertain a woman I don't know, along with her baby. "Sure thing. Do you know where Winifred lives? I live with her."

"I do."

"Come on by around ten, and we'll drink tea and do something very civil where I promise I won't get mad at you over a sweater. You can make as many mistakes as you like, and I won't get angry at all. You can even break my favorite mug, and we'll have a good old laugh about it."

Janet giggles at the scandal. "You don't have to do this. I'm okay. It's just a bad day."

My arm fixes around her so I can squeeze her shoulder while we walk in step down the pavement. "Something tells me you've had enough bad days to be able to appreciate a good one."

Janet exhales into my side, sealing this as the moment the two of us become friends.

MESSY GIRL TIME

The next morning has me sitting at the kitchen table with Karen, while Agnes and Aunt Winnie orbit around us, pleasantly squabbling over how best to tweak the recipe for the thing they are planning on making today.

I let loose a loud guffaw when Karen tells me what I missed when I left Delia's house prematurely. "The letter in the envelope we steamed open was really just an invoice from the lawncare service? All that trouble for nothing? I gave myself a full-on existential crisis!"

Karen chortles at my exacerbation. "You and that do-gooder spirit. It's going to drive you straight off a cliff one of these days."

I grumble in response, then turn to my great-aunt and Agnes, who are still squabbling by the stove while something heats in the big pot. "You're really not telling me what we're making?" I ask Aunt Winnie.

"I'm really, really not. That is, not until Agnes and I can settle on how to get this right this time. I swear, Agnes, we boiled the sugar too hot last time. It didn't have the right consistency."

Agnes rests her fist on her generous hip, sighing with impatience. "It wasn't that it was too hot; it was that it grew too hot too fast. We don't need to adjust the temperature goal; we need to let the sugar heat longer and slower until it reaches the number here in the book."

Aunt Winnie frowns at the spattered and stained cookbook. "We can try that. But the moment it reaches temperature we take it off the heat completely. That very second."

Agnes and Aunt Winnie shake hands, finally coming to an agreement.

"*Now* can I know what we're making?" I motion to a dish in the center of the table that has four sticks of softened butter in the center. "The suspense is reaching critical mass."

Aunt Winnie nods. "We need more hands, first. You said Janet is coming, right?"

"With her baby, yes."

Karen sips her tea, adjusting one of the combs in her hair. "Marianne is on her way. That makes six of us."

As if on cue, the front door opens, and Marianne strolls in with Janet on her heels, toting baby Rachel in a strap-on carrier so her hands are free. "We're here! Let the taffy pulling begin!"

I sit up straighter, light dancing in my eyes. "We're making taffy? I've never done that before!"

Aunt Winnie grins at the unleashing of the secret. "You're going to love it. But you're overdressed. You, too, Janet. And Marianne, I told you to wear clothes you don't care about."

Marianne looks down. "I don't care about this shirt."

"But those are cute shorts."

Agnes takes out several aprons, handing them to us and going so far as to tie Janet's on for her over the baby carrier, so Rachel's little round head pokes out but the rest of her is covered. "I think they're ready, ladies." Agnes speaks with the air of readying for war.

Karen stands and smacks her hands together. "Okay, girls. The name of the game is keeping your hands buttered at all times. Your hair needs to be back, because getting hardened taffy out of your hair is nearly impossible. We have to stretch the taffy once it's heated, and that's a full-body workout."

I don't know what to make of the serious assignment being levied. It all sounds goofy and like something that exists only for fun, which is right up my alley.

Marianne's grin stretches from ear to ear, while Janet looks as if she has stepped into an alternate universe where taffy is highest priority. Marianne slaps her palms together after tying her apron in place. "I'm ready. Butter me up, Karen."

Suddenly the four sticks of softened butter in the center of the table make sense.

Karen holds her hand up, and then removes a comb from her hair. "Not so fast. You've got to push your hair back. Here." Marianne holds still while Karen secures her short hair from her pretty face. "Much better. Janet? Let me get you a ponytail." She trots off and comes back with a rubber band looped around her fingers. Instead of handing it to Janet, Karen stands behind the woman and sweeps her bony fingers through Janet's brown hair, fixing it into a ponytail so Janet doesn't have to do it herself.

I can tell by the way Janet's lashes sweep shut that she is new to being cared for so sweetly. When she opens her eyes again, I can tell she is unused to any of this, but wishes she was.

My heart longs to make things better for Janet. When I invited her over, it was for tea and time out of her house. But when I told the Live Forever Club that she was coming over this morning, they wasted no time making plans to concoct a memorable morning for Janet, who could use the distraction from what sounds like a tumultuous existence.

The six of us dote on Rachel and share fun stories while we wait for the sugar concoction to reach the right temperature. The entire kitchen smells like hot sugar, which is a different experience than what my commercial kitchen smells like when I'm mixing my ingredients. There's a warmth from the smell that feels like a hug in my insides, heating parts of me that I didn't realize needed a little extra tenderness and awakening. I love the kitchen today, mostly because it is filled with the women I adore. I feel this memory imprinting itself in my soul, reminding me that sometimes life can be filled with sugar and silliness, and those are the best kinds of days. I feel like if my heart has room for those two things, then I can't be too far off the mark when it comes to building a life that I love.

While Agnes and Marianne take a softer approach with Janet, easing her in with smiles and compliments, Karen takes the more direct route. "I'm glad you're here, Janet. You look like you could use a little girl time." She motions around the interior of the home. "This is a safe space, you know. You can be yourself here. You can spill things. You can have loud opinions. You can let your shoulders ease up."

Janet takes in a deep breath and finally lets her shoulders loose, her posture going from erect to relaxed. "Sorry. This is all a bit new to me. I always see you having fun together. I didn't realize that it's just how you are all the time—not a smile that comes out at town events. This is really what you're doing today? We're making taffy?" She looks as if her elation might finally begin to overtake her nerves.

Aunt Winnie beams proudly. "Sometimes we forget that the most important moments are the unimportant ones. Those are the moments in which we live. The more you do it, the more addictive it all becomes. Trust me, after today, you'll start looking for fun instead of being confused when it finds you."

My great-aunt is entirely correct, because that is exactly how it was for me when I moved here. Fun wasn't a high priority, but in a short time, I've learned not to balk at the crucial parts of life that have managed to find me here in Sweetwater Falls with these amazing women.

Janet's voice sounds small, like it needs convincing to come out and play. "I think I used to be fun. It's been so long."

Karen drapes an arm around Janet's shoulders and gives her a bolstering squeeze. "Well, after today, you won't be able to say that anymore."

Once the sugar reaches the correct temperature, Aunt Winnie jerks the pot off the burner and sets it on a heating pad atop the counter. "Okay, ladies. It's time to butter your hands. This taffy needs a good stretch, or it'll be a lump of sugar. We want silky taffy. We want it to melt in your mouth and stick to your teeth just long enough to make a good memory. If we get this right, we can package it up and hand out taffy for the entire town."

I straighten at the assignment, not realizing that this taffy was meant for more than just us. Now I really want to get this right. "I've never stretched taffy before. Is there a trick to it? A method to keep things going well?"

Agnes reaches into the pot with a buttered wooden

spoon and scoops out a lump of the concoction that we have decided should be dyed a bright pink. There's a glassy sheen to it, instead of the crayon-bold pink that I've seen at stores. This is homemade taffy, and it looks like a blob of art atop wax paper. Agnes is the tester, so the moment she declares it cool enough to touch, she picks up the lump and slaps it into Marianne's buttered palms.

I'm working my way up to buttering my hands. I don't know how to do this without immediately wanting to scratch my face, which seems like the last thing you would want to do when your hands are slathered so thoroughly. Taking Marianne's grimace as an indicator that more butter is better in this situation, I lock eyes with the equally unsure Janet, and the two of us reach for a handful of butter. The squishy feel of the fat all over my hands isn't unpleasant, but so much of my job goes into not tracking fats, flours and sugars all over the kitchen that to purposefully oil myself up is contrary to my usual purpose. Still, I dig in, making sure that, if I'm going to learn to pull taffy, I'm going to go all the way without holding back.

Janet blanches at the squelch of the butter between her fingers, but to her credit, she goes back in for another pinch off the stick in the center of the table when she worries she's missed a spot. "This is the most disgusting thing I've done all day, and I've changed three diapers already this morning."

Agnes chortles as she slops the second pink scoop into Janet's hands, smiling when Janet's closed-mouth shriek lets us know that she is far outside of her comfort zone, but she is here for the wild ride. After plopping a softball-sized lump in my hands, Agnes takes two fingers and swirls them in the air over her head. "Okay, girls. Pair up with one of us, and let's start stretching!"

Aunt Winnie stands across from me, Agnes locks eyes with Marianne, and Karen's buttered fingers wiggle at Janet. Baby Rachel coos while the Live Forever Club reaches out and pulls on the balls of taffy in our hands, yanking the stretchy sugar out, and then folding it back into our palms. Another stretch, and over again. The taffy is gooey and warm, slipping through my fingers often enough that I let out a shriek.

Marianne giggles so loud, I am certain she is verging on hysterical.

"I can't! It's so slippery! I'm going to drop it, but it's so sticky! Ah!" Marianne loses her footing, stepping on a slick part of the floor from an errant chunk of butter. Her feet slide out from under her, and just like that, Marianne is giggling on the floor, staring up at Agnes. "Ouch!"

Agnes tries to offer a hand to lift Marianne up, but they're both so slippery that Marianne only makes it to her knees before she slips again, this time landing on her stomach on the kitchen floor. "Careful!" Agnes and I cry out to her, but Marianne is lost to her giggles, engulfed by the silliness that found us all at just the right time.

Marianne has butter and food coloring all over her arms, legs and face, and she couldn't be happier. She laughs so hard on the floor that she cries, holding her stomach while she howls.

This causes baby Rachel to stare at her curiously, as if to ask Marianne which one of them is the child. "I can't get up! I'm..." She lets out a loud sigh through her laughter. "I needed this so badly. I got all fidgety about an argument with Carlos, when it turns out, all he wanted to know is whether or not we wanted to move in together someday. I've been on the fence about it, but now that I'm on the floor, covered in slime, what was I so scared of? Why wouldn't I want to move in with him? It doesn't have to happen right now. It can be whenever we're both ready for that kind of thing. It's okay that I'm not ready now. It's just exciting that the option exists."

Agnes stands over Marianne with her hands on her hips, a look of sheer frustration on her face. "If it takes pulling taffy with you until you can finally make peace with your feelings, then we're going to have a lot of candy around the house. I hope you realize you're allowed to state your truth, young lady. You don't have to run from conflict just because you're afraid you might disagree with Carlos. He's a good man. And if you can't tell him you're not ready right now, but you might be someday, then why bother being with him? He's okay taking it slow with you. You just have to keep your head about you and talk to the man."

Marianne's laughter is still accompanied by tears. She lays flat on her back and pretends to swim on the kitchen floor, tangling her short hair in the butter streaks on the linoleum. "I think part of me knows that, but the other part is afraid to disappoint him by saying I'm not ready to move in with him yet."

Agnes towers over Marianne. "If the man you're with can't handle himself through a little disappointment, then he's not the man for you. Understood?"

Marianne nods, wiping butter across her face as she tries to swipe the tears from her cheeks. "I do now. And next time, I'll talk to him without being so nervous about it. He's a good guy. I just don't like letting people down."

"The only person you have to worry about disappointing is yourself. This decision not to move in with him —is it what you want?"

Marianne nods, still lying on the floor. "I love him, but I'm not ready to move in. I like things a little together and a little separate. I'm pretty sure I don't want to move in with a man unless we're getting married."

I can tell Marianne didn't understand she felt that way because the moment she utters those words, her eyes grow wide and her breath sucks in sharply. I get to watch in real time as my best friend realizes that Carlos is indeed the man she someday would like to marry.

It's a beautiful thing, and the fact that this momentous revelation is sanctioned by butter and sugar only makes it that much sweeter.

Agnes nods, satisfied that finally Marianne is listening

to herself, instead of apologizing for taking up space in this world.

It's a skill Janet has not learned in the slightest.

Every few seconds, I hear Janet's meek, "Oops! I'm sorry, Karen. I think I was off on that one." The apologies fly out of Janet as easy as breathing.

While Agnes has known Marianne long enough to be able to correct her with the harsh truth, Janet is new to our circle, so when Karen points this out, she does so gently. "Janet dear, you know you don't have to apologize for the taffy being too slick to hold well. That's sort of the whole point of this."

Janet nods. "You're right. I'm sorry."

Karen's mouth firms. "I'll make you a deal. You get to apologize for punching me in the face, but nothing else. Understood?"

"What?" Janet asks while Marianne giggles, still on the floor. "I would never do that!"

"Good. Then you don't get to apologize until that day comes. Not for anything short of punching me in the face. I think that's a good line to set."

Janet tilts her head at Karen, as if the spry old woman is the strangest bird Janet has ever seen. "But I should apologize if I do something wrong."

Karen shakes her head. "Actually, you apologize if you do something wicked or hurtful. Dropping the taffy is neither of those things. It's okay to be a person, even if it's only in this house. One day, you'll have enough practice at imperfection around us that you carry that confidence outside these four walls." Karen leans in with a sparkle of affection in her eyes. "I look forward to that day, Janet the Courageous."

My heart swells as this day christens itself with importance. My nickname from the Live Forever Club is Charlotte the Brave. Marianne is Marianne the Wild. Janet the Courageous is just the right blessing for the woman who looks to be frightened of her own shadow, and certainly afraid of her own voice.

I twist at the waist and reach over to hug her, but instead of gifting her some affection, an uncouth screech belts out of me when my foot hits a slick spot, and my legs fly out from under me. My chin hits the floor, but just like Marianne, I can't stop laughing, even as discomfort vibrates up my face and jaw. This is the best day I've had in a while, and certainly the most ridiculous.

I'm grateful I have a new friend to share in the silliness —a new friend to practice courage with, so we can step more boldly out the front door the next time the world tries to tell us we should be small and silent.

13

QUEEN KAREN'S ROYAL RULE

*C*leaning the kitchen is an impossible task, given that Karen, Agnes, Aunt Winnie, Marianne, Janet and I are covered in butter and bits of sticky taffy from head to toe. The only one who has escaped the mayhem is the baby, who has a tea towel over her head to shield her from our insanity. I take the first shower, only because I am determined to take first crack at degreasing the kitchen. I lay out clean clothes for Marianne and Janet, deciding that, even though it is only two o'clock, the six of us are going to indulge in a pajama day.

Janet is all giggles and smiles until she calls home to let her husband know that she will be staying later than the assumed couple hours of tea with me that we'd planned.

"Let's make it a slumber party," Marianne suggests as she towel-dries her hair in the entryway from the living room to the kitchen.

I point to her feet. "Do not step a toe in this area, young lady, otherwise we'll have to de-butter you all over again."

Marianne grins as she lifts her foot and waves it over the kitchen floor, readying to take a step just to taunt me. Then she retracts it with a snicker. "I'll resist. I think I bruised my butt with that last fall. No fun."

"Well, I had fun watching you be ridiculous," I admit. "You're in a good mood. I can tell there's been a shift from last week to this one."

Marianne frizzes her hair with the towel once more. "You're partly responsible for that. The system you suggested for the charity drive has made the whole thing less of a chore. I think I wanted to fight with something, so I chose that instead of seeing the obvious solution that would make everything easier."

"It happens. I'm glad you're you again."

Marianne opens her mouth to respond, but Janet's clipped worry to her husband on the phone filters through the air. "I'm sorry, Charles. I didn't realize. Of course, I can come home and cook your dinner. You're right. I didn't think."

Karen moseys in from the hallway where Aunt Winnie's bedroom rests, her shoulders back and her wet hair dampening none of her moxie. "Let me see that." It's a command, not a suggestion. Karen lifts the phone from Janet's grip with the air of a queen retrieving her scepter. "Charles? How old are you, young man?"

I can hear a mumbled reply that I can't make out.

"Good. Then I assume you can heat up a can of soup, assemble a salad or take this very phone that you're speaking to me on right now and order a pizza?" Another pause, and then Karen answers with a strict, "I prefer you call me 'ma'am'. When I ask you a simple question, you may respond with 'Yes, ma'am.'" Karen waits for the greeting she approves of and then speaks as if she is doling out commands from her throne. "When was the last time Janet had a girls' night?"

The silence needs no amplification. We can all guess that Janet has not had a girls' night since she got married. Her last night out was probably long before that.

"Then you can thank me for remedying that oversight. It matters to you that your wife smiles, yes?"

I love that Karen frames everything by making agreeing with her edict the only logical response.

"Good. Janet and Rachel are having a girls' night here. I trust you are competent enough to feed yourself? Or will Rachel learn that skill before you?"

Janet is rocking Rachel, tears streaming down her cheeks as she whispers, "It's really fine, Karen. Honest."

Karen is having none of it. "Good. Janet and Rachel will be home around noon tomorrow. I trust by then you will have learned to speak kindly and regard your wife with respect." When her narrowed eyes fall on Janet's distress, I see a plan forming in her mind. "Actually, I'm going to come with her tomorrow. My hip is giving me problems, and I need help, being that I'm old and fragile."

Agnes chortles quietly as she joins the fray in her red flannel nightgown after emerging from her shower. To hear Karen refer to herself as old and fragile is a joke only Karen herself can get away with telling, because one look at her bony, thin frame when paired with the burning passion in her eyes is enough to tell the world that she will always be capable and filled with vitality.

Karen reaches over and squeezes Janet's elbow. "I need looking after, and I trust very few people. I'll need to stay with Janet for a few days until I get on my feet. Plus, if you need her to come home from a good time just to cook your dinner, I'm guessing you could use a few cooking lessons, which I will be happy to provide. You have a cot you can put out for me, yes?"

Janet nods through her tears, in awe of the plan Karen is concocting on the fly.

It's one thing to stand up to a friend's husband once but sticking around to ensure he doesn't ream her out for letting Karen speak to him like this takes a third presence in the room to remind Charles that he needs to be on his best behavior.

He's not going to be able to blame Janet for all the problems in the world tomorrow. In fact, if Karen has her way, he'll learn how to treat Janet with the respect she deserves by the week's end.

Karen reaches her arm out after Agnes takes Rachel from her grip. And just like that, Janet folds her body into Karen's, sobbing audibly once Karen ends the call. "It's going to be okay," Karen tells her. And because it's Karen, I believe that this hopeless situation now has a ray of light to cling to.

Janet cries into Karen's thin shoulder, drawing strength from the wiry woman's bravery. "I can't believe you just did that. You're really going to come over and stay? He's so angry at me! I knew he wouldn't let me stay the night here."

"Ah, but you're here, aren't you? Do you want to stay the night and have some girl time, or would you rather go home?"

I can tell even through the reddened puffiness around Janet's eyes that she very much wants to stay, but the cost of one night of freedom might be too steep a price to pay. But now that Karen will be coming home with her tomorrow, the fallout will be limited. Janet lets loose a marriage-worth of tears into Karen's blue silk camisole and short set that I got her for Christmas. After a few minutes of Agnes cooing to Rachel and Karen holding Janet, the sobs turn to hiccups and sniffles, and finally, Janet's anxiety quells.

Marianne shakes her head. "I would never let a man talk to me the way Charles speaks to you. You were right to stand up to him, Janet."

Karen, in her infinite wisdom, corrects Marianne's words. "Actually, you have no idea what you would tolerate when you are newly married, and you have a baby to look after." It's a gentle cover of protection Karen drapes over Janet, making it clear that she is in a safe place, and Karen will go with her wherever Janet's path leads. She kisses Janet's cheek as she releases her from the hug. "I heard talk of a movie night, which means we'll need snacks. I'm not sure I can tolerate a taste of the taffy just yet. I think there's still some stuck behind my ear. But I wouldn't say no to some popcorn."

Aunt Winnie raises her hand as she comes out from her bedroom, freshly showered in her nightgown and robe. "On it!"

I get down on my hands and knees, scrubbing the grease from the linoleum to ensure that none of the precious ladies in my life slip on this near perfect night. Marianne orders a few pizzas so we can all relax into the evening, which will be dominated by popcorn, Cary Grant, and the best women in the universe.

14

A NEW FRIEND

Marianne and I slept in the living room on sleeping bags so Janet and Rachel could share my bedroom. After the emotional purging Janet did last night, I figured she could use a nice, soft mattress to cradle her to sleep.

The two of us wake when we hear Rachel stirring, and without a word, we start making breakfast for the women we love. Marianne and I move around each other in the kitchen seamlessly, with Marianne making coffee and cutting the tops off the strawberries while I scramble ten eggs in the frying pan.

It's a strange thing to be so wholly content. It's like catching yourself before a fall, only to realize that you're in no danger of toppling in the slightest. A deep breath fills my lungs, reminding me that this is a special existence, this life in this home with these women in this sweet, small town I adore. I could have ended up married to a man who is unkind, and the beauty of this place would be lost on me as a result.

The women come out one by one, stretching and yawning because we stayed up far too late giggling about the plot of the movie while we reenacted our favorite scenes. Karen had thrown popcorn at us if the acting wasn't cheesy enough.

The six of us plus Rachel play cards over breakfast, laughing about the various things we've discovered while sorting through the donations for the charity drive.

Marianne shakes her head through her snickering. "I mean, why would you keep, let alone donate, a beach towel with a giant hole in the middle?"

Aunt Winnie chortles, adding her own finds to the fire. "I found a butter knife that was bent in half. Why? How? And why donate it? Never in my life have I gone thrifting in hopes of finding a butter knife bent into a hoop."

Janet snorts when she giggles, which is entirely endearing. Karen feeds her bites of scrambled eggs while she nurses Rachel at the table. It's incredible to watch how closely Karen and Janet have latched onto each other. It's like watching a flower opening its petals in the dawning of springtime. I can tell this is the most Janet has smiled and exhaled in many years. It looks good on her— even better than the borrowed sweatpants and t-shirt that are swimming on someone nearly half a foot shorter than me.

When Marianne stands, Agnes rises to kiss her cheek. "Heading off to the library?"

Marianne takes another sip of her coffee before washing her dishes off in the sink and then sticking them in the dishwasher. "Yep. I'm a bit behind, since I spent the bulk of my time last week at the charity drive."

"Need help sorting books?" I ask, volunteering myself for the task I never mind helping her with at the library. Marianne has done so much to help launch my business that I jump on any opportunity to return the favor.

"I wouldn't say no to an hour of that. Thanks, Charlotte. And Janet, I'm putting aside a children's book for Rachel that I think you'll love reading to her. Stop by the library before you and Karen head to your place?"

Janet beams at Marianne. "Really? That's so nice. Thank you."

Karen feeds Janet another bite after Janet resituates Rachel on her other side. "Do you enjoy reading, Janet?"

The woman nods, but then gives a regretful smile. "I do, but I haven't had much time for it. You know, newborn life."

Karen turns her chin to Marianne. "Mind putting something aside for Janet, too? I haven't held Rachel long enough. Everyone keeps hogging the baby. I have a feeling I'll want to play with the baby all afternoon—long enough for Janet to read a few chapters that might refuel her soul."

Marianne's posture lifts as she goes into librarian mode. "Absolutely!" Whenever someone shows an interest in reading, my best friend comes to life. "What genre would you like? Maybe a shorter length, so you don't have to worry about completing it."

Janet gapes at all of us. "Is this what it's like to have girlfriends? You do this sort of thing for each other? Get each other books, and then make sure they have time to get read?"

Aunt Winnie nods firmly. "Anything you need, this is the place to say it." She motions to me. "Charlotte brings me home extra cupcakes every week. I'm telling you; I never ate so good."

Agnes dips her chin to Aunt Winnie. "Winifred repaired one of my chipped planter pots while I was out with Gus last week. Sneaked in, the devious minx, and superglued it perfectly in place. It looked so good, I thought I'd gone crazy and imagined the crack."

Karen waves her hand at Marianne and me. "These two drive me around whenever I need a lift. I don't even have to ask. They just show up and never make me feel like a burden."

I scoff at the notion. "You could never be a burden. It's partially selfish, anyway. I pick you up, and you tell me how pretty my hair looks. I swear, sometimes I drive you around extra on days I need the pick-me-up."

Karen chuckles at me while Marianne reaches out to cup Janet's shoulder. "A picture book for Rachel, and something fun for you. Got any preferences?"

Janet looks so overwhelmed with the gift of being given

time and a choice that when she opens her mouth, she gets all tongue-tied. "I think... I used to like reading prairie novels, but maybe I should try something new. Nothing scary. Something with a happy ending?"

Marianne smiles at our new friend. "I know just the thing." Then she blows us all a kiss and makes her way out the front door.

Whenever Janet looks down at Rachel to adjust the baby's position, her hair falls forward, and she has to sweep it back from her face. After I finish my breakfast, I stick my dishes and Aunt Winnie's into the dishwasher and then head to my bedroom, retrieving two hair ties that I think will look nice with Janet's brown shoulder-length locks. While Karen and Janet make plans for the day, I comb Janet's hair back so the world can see her face. Then I do my best attempt at two French braids running down either side of her head, so her hair doesn't fall forward anymore.

The change is drastic, and exactly what Janet needs. I can see it in the faces of the Live Forever Club, who smile covertly over their cups of coffee when they can finally take in the unobscured features of the woman who makes it her life's goal to be invisible and apologize for taking up the least amount of space. When I go to leave for the library to help Marianne out for an hour or two, Aunt Winnie catches my hand, giving it a light squeeze. "You're my angel. You know that, right?"

I kiss the top of my great-aunt's head, grateful that she

took the time to pull me out of my shell, just as Karen is setting about to do for Janet.

If Janet's life is changed in any way similar to how mine has been altered, then I know that Janet is about to come alive, perhaps for the very first time.

15

POPS AND PLOTS

*I*t's a hot day out, which makes me grateful that the ovens aren't going to be in use at the Bravery Bakery this morning. I don't want to be sweating through my clothes half an hour into my workday. Betty is off this coming week to celebrate her anniversary, which means that I need to stay on top of my orders, or I will be massively behind. I can't exactly ask Logan to come over and help me whip up the frosting, either, because he is elbow-deep in an unsolvable murder investigation where the clues have stopped adding up to anything that might prove useful.

Today I am making cake pops, which means that the leftover cupcakes from last week come out of the freezer and go into my giant mixing bowl, where they are crumbled by hand into a mess of flavors that are each good on their own, but together they make a whole new flavor that you just can't beat. A few months ago, I decided to expand my business to make cake pops, which would only be sold at various businesses around Sweetwater Falls. Each business has their own design, so people can only purchase the gemstone cake pops at Sweetwater Fountains. The "Extra! Extra!" cake pops can only be purchased at the Nosy Newsy, and so on. It was a fantastic idea, but with the summer tourists come a deluge of orders. Each business requires at least double their normal amount of confections, which is exciting for all our businesses, but takes more time and elbow grease than I have after dozing off on the living room floor in a sleeping bag.

No matter. I sing to my goldfish, who never minds that I occasionally go off-key, while I turn cupcakes to crumb and add in unhealthy dollops of frosting. I always make sure to have extra bowls of buttercream on hand. It's a beautiful thing to squish my fingers in the mess, combining the ingredients until they are the right consistency to be formed into golf ball sized spheres without being too sticky or losing their shape altogether. My music plays through the kitchen for hours while I melt the chocolate and then dip my beautiful little pops into the gooey sweetness. The entire kitchen smells like happiness, and after a night like the one I shared with my girlfriends, I am fairly certain that nothing could wipe the smile from my face.

It takes hours for everything to be made, then decorated and packaged up, but I manage the feat without the help of my favorite baking assistant. Betty took it upon herself to make an extra batch of frosting, so I had a bit of a head start without her. It's the little extra things Betty does that reminds me how grateful I am to have someone like her in my corner. Though, now that I am sweating and running low on the crucial pep in my step as I load up my red sedan with my deliveries, I wonder if I couldn't use a second baking assistant every now and then to make things easier.

That's a question for another day, as I have to make good time on my deliveries, or the chocolate might melt, and the hard work I did making such beautiful designs will have been for nothing. That is not the afternoon I would like to have.

I love that I've added several businesses to my route. It makes me happy to spend face time with the businessowners, knowing that I am one of them. I cannot believe how many people I know by name now, and how often I can ask them a question about their life because we have a plethora of past conversations to pull from.

Even though my feet are dragging as I make my way through the town, my soul is filled with the smiles that greet me along the way. When I reach the Nosy Newsy, my smile falters. Again, Dwight is manning the kiosk, though this time in a different mascot costume.

I wave him down and set the box on his small counter beside the register. "I've got to ask, Dwight. Is there a market for giant banana mascot costumes? I know you make these for yourself, and you sell them online. Do you get many orders for big bananas?"

Dwight grins at me. "The more I wear a costume and take pictures of myself doing normal things in it and post those photos on my website and on social media, the more that costume sells. I wait until I've got a few dozen made, then I wear that costume out and about. It's a decent system. I checked my online orders at lunch today, and I've already got five. There will be more after I post the rest of my pictures this evening. Take another photo for me?"

He hands me his phone and then pops open the box of cake pops, plucking one out and holding it to his mouth as if he's about to munch on it. I snap a few photos from different angles, wondering how many other people have been asked to help Dwight with such a task. "That should do it." I motion to the booth with a frown after handing back his phone. "Frank is still out of town?"

Dwight nods, setting out the cake pops on a special spot on the stand near the register. "Yep. He called yesterday, asking me to work here all week for him. It's great business for me, really. I get to wear my costumes out and about and sell a lot of my inventory in the process. My giant egg costume never sells, but I'm wearing that one tomorrow to see if I can clear out my backstock. Fingers crossed."

I make a show of crossing my fingers to wish him good luck, but my mind is elsewhere. "Did Frank mention where he was going? It's odd that he would take off for days on end and not tell anyone where he was headed."

Dwight shrugs, which moves the giant banana costume up by a few inches, brushing the top on the overhang. "He didn't tell me. Said it was personal, and that he wasn't sure how long he'd be gone. I feel bad for the guy. I'm having the time of my life, and he's probably off handling something difficult. Sounded all serious on the phone." Dwight turns to a passerby and salutes them. "Evening, young lady. Did you remember to get your potassium today?"

I wait until I have Dwight's attention once more. "Could you call him? I don't have Frank's phone number. I'm worried about him." Or, more accurately, I'm worried about him being a coldblooded killer and possibly fleeing town to escape the law. It's odd to need time away from the town for personal, unspecified reasons right after a severed hand shows up and his girlfriend goes missing. I don't want Frank to be a suspect, but I like even less the idea of him disappearing before I can cross him off my list of possible deviants.

Dwight pulls out his phone and shows me Frank's number. "There you go." Then he tilts his head at me, and the whole costume moves a little bit with the motion. "What's got you worried?"

I don't want to spread uncertainty through the town, but Dwight's caught me at just the right moment for my vulnerability to shine through what I was hoping would be a chipper exterior. "Delia was supposed to be home days ago, but no one's heard from her. Now Frank takes off?"

"Maybe they're spending some time together. I know that's what Frank wants. He's always trying to get more time in with Delia."

"Yeah. That's probably it." I don't want to tell Dwight that that's exactly what I'm afraid of. Normally, I'd be thrilled to think of the two of them scurrying away to have a bit of time together. But I can't shake the concern that we still don't have the killer nailed down, and right now, Frank is the most likely suspect.

I feel horrible for even thinking that. I don't want to assume the worst of a friend who has been nothing but kind to me. I also can't shake the fact that he lied about his whereabouts the weekend before the hand was found, he was at the scene of the crime, and now his girlfriend is missing from Sweetwater Falls.

Dwight purses his lips in my direction. "Hey, Frank's okay. He called me to ask me to work the stand for him a bit longer. I heard his voice, and he didn't sound like he was on death's door or anything, if that's what's got you all twisted up."

I feign a cheery expression that fools neither of us, then thank Dwight for his time. "That's good to hear. I'll see you around."

I drive off after calling Frank's number and getting no response. Then I decide to reach out to the one person who will never make me justify the need to vent about a case that's gone unsolved.

"Good evening, Miss Charlotte."

I don't realize what needs to happen until I hear his voice. Then my mind shoots in a single direction and won't settle for waiting around a moment longer. "Hi, Logan. Feel like a road trip?"

16

ROAD TRIP

I'm sure an evening spent with my boyfriend could be more romantic than the two of us separated by the console while I drive us out of town. We head north with no plan of stopping anytime soon. We could be on a date, or walking through the town, talking about life, and making doe-eyed plans for the future. However, tonight Logan sits in the passenger's seat of my car, holding my hand without questioning me in the slightest.

"You're a good friend," I tell him yet again. "You just said yes to losing half a night of sleep on a whim."

"You're making me sound entirely too altruistic. You're forgetting that I'm partly here for selfish reasons. I get to spend time with you, which is always the top item on my master plan."

"Then I fell right into your web," I say with a smirk.

"You realize I'm nuts, right? You should stop me from crossing state lines."

Logan laughs airily through his nose. "Oh no! Stop! Don't care about your friends."

My left hand tightens on the steering wheel as rush hour finds us on the freeway. "Delia hasn't answered any of Betty's texts or my calls. She has a turtle and didn't call Betty to check that she could feed it if she stayed away a few more days. She would have called, Logan."

"So, you used a cupcake to bribe the information out of Betty, getting the address of Delia's mother's home, where she went for the week. Totally logical and not evil at all."

I can't tell if he's joking or not. "I know I shouldn't be bothering Delia while she's out of town, but Betty and I are worried about her. Frank didn't murder that person and put their hand in the jar. I refuse to believe that happened."

Logan gives my denial a few beats to settle in the air. "If you refuse to believe it, then tell me why we're driving three hours out of town on a whim."

I close my eyes when the traffic around us comes to a stop. "I'm a terrible person."

Logan squeezes my hand. "Ease up on yourself. We haven't been able to identify who the hand belonged to. For what it's worth, I requested Delia's fingerprints be run against the hand you found. If it's her, then we can give ourselves permission to worry worse than we are now."

I balk at him. "You think the missing hand is from Delia? You think Delia is dead?"

Logan's brows crease. "Isn't that what you're hinting at?"

"That's exactly what I'm trying *not* to hint at!" But it's what I've been thinking. Still, I don't want it said aloud. That makes it more real. "I'm still trying to digest the idea that Frank murdered someone, but not Delia! You think he murdered Delia?"

Logan holds up his free hand. "I don't have the slightest idea who was murdered or who did the killing. But if we've got a missing woman and a severed hand that looks like it belonged to a woman, then I'm not going to ignore those two puzzle pieces just because I don't like that they might fit together."

I stare ahead at the unmoving cars, wishing now more than ever that the traffic would clear up so we can make sure that exactly what Logan described didn't actually happen. "I don't want to make that connection. You think Delia could really be dead?"

"I'm hoping she's just missing a hand. And if she is gone, then yes, Frank is the most likely suspect. But one step at a time, Miss Charlotte. I'm hoping we pull up to Delia's mom's house and she is sitting there, perfectly fine. Maybe her phone broke, and she hasn't been able to get calls or texts. There's a logical explanation for all of it, even if the direction is looking more clearly to be something sinister."

We wait for the traffic to clear up in silence, unwilling to add more fire to the flames of suspicion and dread. I don't want any of this to be true, so I send out my best optimism, however feeble it may be at this point, and hope beyond hope that Frank is the good man I believe him to be, and that Delia's phone just happens to be broken.

Because the alternative is not an option I can bear.

Twilight is setting in when we reach the address Betty gave me. It's a small ranch home with freshly mown grass and a giant plastic daisy on the mailbox. I suck in a deep breath and summon my bravery as I step out of the car with Logan by my side. We walk together to the porch, and I feel my breath quickening. "If Delia's not here, are we going to make her mother worry?"

Logan shrugs as he presses his finger to the doorbell. "It's too late to turn back now."

But when the front door opens, neither Delia nor her mother stand in the entryway to greet us. Instead, the tall form of Frank regards us with a wariness that's mixed with confusion. "Logan? Charlotte? What are you two doing here?"

17

DELIA'S MOTHER

I had a plan for if Delia answered the door when we showed up unannounced at her mother's house. I was going to throw my arms around her, relieved that's she's alive. I also had a plan for if her mother answered the door. I was going to introduce myself and ask if she'd seen Delia recently, because I couldn't get ahold of her.

But when Frank stands in the doorway, his mouth drawn in a tight line of disapproval, all words desert me.

Fortunately, Logan is not as tongue-tied. "Evening, Frank. Good to see you."

"Weird to see you," Frank replies, reaching out to shake Logan's hand. "You two just happen to find yourselves in the neighborhood or something? It's a far cry from Sweetwater Falls."

It was my idea to come here, my plan to confront the unsolved mystery head on. But now that I am here, I've gone mute.

Logan plasters on a breezy smile. "We didn't know you would be here, actually. See, Delia told Betty she'd be back a few days ago, and no one's heard from her since. We were worried, what with the events at the charity drive."

Frank studies us for a few beats and then his eyes grow wide. "Oh! You're worried that the hand you found might belong to Delia? That's why you're here—to check on her to make sure she's okay?"

I exhale, nodding emphatically as if our plan was exactly that simple. "Yes. Is she here?"

Frank nods, standing to the side to usher us in. "Right this way."

The place smells like an old diaper that's been filled many times over. There are flies in the house that have no fear of humans as they buzz around our faces. There are stains on the wall and something sticky on the carpet as we walk further in. Something is very wrong here.

Logan grips my hand to keep me by his side, knowing that if Frank is the killer, coming into the house is the wrong move. "Delia!" Logan calls through the house, loud enough for the neighbors to hear him and alert them to our presence, should we need that kind of assurance if things go south.

"That's real good of you two. Delia's been a little out of

sorts, you see. Her mother, well, she took a turn and it's been hard on my sweet Delia. You really came all the way out here to check on her?"

I throw Frank a light smile. "Of course." But as we walk down the hallway, I see no signs of Delia or her mother. There's a walker beside a recliner, and what looks like a carpet stain that was once a pool of blood, now poorly cleaned and dried. I hold Logan's hand tighter, and he nods at the stain, letting me know that he is aware that this trip might come to a bitter end sooner rather than later.

My stomach churns as Frank directs us to the last room on the right, where I am not sure what we might find waiting for us inside. My voice comes out in a choked whisper as fear overtakes me. "Delia? Delia, where are you?"

When we turn into the bedroom that is lit only by a dim lamp, I nearly faint at the very normal sight that greets us.

"Delia?" Logan says, just as shocked as I am that we haven't been marching to our own deaths.

And there she is, sitting in a rocking chair beside a single bed where an elderly woman sleeps with an IV hooked to her arm. Delia's mouth pops open in surprise when she takes in the sight of us in her mother's bedroom. "Um, hi? What's going on? What are you two doing way out here?"

Logan recovers quicker than I can manage. "We

wanted to make sure you were okay." He keeps his voice low and motions to the hallway. "I don't want to wake your mother."

Frank raises his hand and comes into the room. "I'll sit with her. Go on to the living room."

Delia follows us to the front room, which is small, housing only a recliner and a loveseat that looks older than I am. She plops in her mother's recliner and motions for us to take the loveseat. "What are you two doing out here?"

Logan is calm and quiet as he explains the severed hand that I found at the charity drive. "No one's heard from you in well over a week, and Betty was starting to worry when you didn't come home. You weren't returning her calls. We wanted to make sure you had both your hands about you, which I can see you clearly do."

Delia slumps forward, her elbows atop her thighs while she cradles her head in her hands with a heavy sigh. "I can't believe you two came all the way out here to check on me. I'm so sorry I didn't get back to Betty. Someone really found a hand in a cookie jar?"

I raise my hand. "I did. I'm glad it wasn't yours."

Delia shudders. "That's disgusting. I thought oatmeal raisin cookies were the worst thing you could find inside a cookie jar, but I guess I was wrong." She takes in a long breath. "But no, I'm not in danger. Betty's been taking care of Michelangelo?"

I nod, waiting for some sort of reason why she couldn't reach out to Betty, and what's taken her so long out here. "She's worried about you. What can I tell her?"

Delia scrubs her hands over her face. I can tell she is tired from the stoop of her shoulders and the lack of pep she usually has on hand. "Tell her that I'm sorry I haven't been checking my phone. Honestly, I don't think I've left the house in a week. I didn't realize it's been so long. Tell her thank you for feeding Michelangelo, and that I'll come home soon."

I lean forward, worried about something other than her murder, now that that matter's been settled. "Delia, what's going on? You look exhausted."

Moisture glistens in her eyes, visible to me even in the dim lamplight. "I am. Lucky that Frank's here, really." She sniffles and shakes her head at the swing of emotion that has her in its grip. "I can't believe him. When I got here, I told him that my mom was worse off than I realized. She's been living in filth for who knows how long without anyone to take care of her. I talk to her on the phone a few times a week, and she always sounds fine. Flighty, but fine. I didn't realize how bad it was until I got here." Delia dabs at her cheek as her shoulders begin to quake. "When I came, my mom was wandering around in her bathrobe, not bathed or changed in who knows how long. The garbage was overflowing and there were ants and flies everywhere. I had no idea she was living like this!"

When a sob breaks loose, I move off the couch and wrap my arms around her to give her a safe place to break down. "That's so scary, Delia."

"Dementia," Delia confirms. "She got the diagnosis months ago and never told me. She can't live like this! I don't know what to do. I'm so overwhelmed. Completely lost. It breaks my heart to think that the woman who raised me wasn't being cared for. I had no idea!"

Logan moves to her other side, his hand on her back to offer his support. "How could you have known?"

Delia sniffles into my shirt while I hold her, stooped over the recliner. "I called Frank, completely at a loss, and he didn't miss a beat. He left his newsstand and came here that day. The place was a mess, and he's been working around the clock to clean it for her while I've been talking with her doctors and taking her to missed appointments. He's amazing. I'm telling you; I don't know what I would have done without him here to help us. To care about me is one thing, but to look after my mother the way he has?" She shakes her head. "He's the best man I've ever known!"

My heart settles into the same rhythm, letting me know that part of me was always on that page. It felt wrong to single out Frank as the bad guy, like a crime against nature to suspect him of anything but kindness. "He's one of the good ones. I'm so glad you have him to lean on."

Logan scratches Delia's back, and I can tell by the way his posture sags that he is just as relieved that Frank is a good man, and Delia is very much alive. "We're here now. Put us to work. I can tackle the carpet. That'll give your mom something nice to walk on when she's up in the morning."

Delia turns her head toward Logan. "How? She doesn't have a carpet cleaner."

"I can go rent one from the nearest hardware store." He checks the clock on the wall. "Mind if I step out and grab one real quick before they close?"

"You're seriously here and you're going to help us?"

I squeeze Delia tighter. "Of course. Give me a list of things to tackle around the house, and you go rest. Frank can watch your mom. Logan and I can look after the house."

Delia cries louder, holding me until her tears run dry for the moment. I can tell she's been trying to keep herself together longer than she can withstand, given the circumstances. "Thank you. I don't know what else to say. Thank you."

I help Delia to the only bedroom in the house. She doesn't have anywhere else to sleep, but neither her mother nor she minds one bit that the two of them will be sharing a bed for the night. Frank and I tuck Delia in beside her mother, who looks as though she's had a bath recently. I kiss Delia's forehead and turn off the lamp.

Frank remains in the rocking chair by the bedside, watching over the mother and daughter while they drift off to sleep.

Frank is a standup guy and is certainly not our killer. While I am relieved to be so very disproven, a niggling thought remains that we still do not have any leads as to who could have done something so terrible.

18

CLEANING AND SELF-LOATHING

I try to keep my movements quiet while I start in the living room, doing what I can do give the house a deep clean. The flies are annoying, but I know that once we take away whatever is attracting them, they will be gone. With love in my heart and determination in my veins, I start from the top down, grabbing several clean rags from the hallway closet so I can dust everything on the walls and shelves, and then polish the table so it's clean enough to shine when the sunlight hits it in the morning.

The curtains are stained, so I take them down and throw them into the washing machine, texting Logan to pick up a container of laundry detergent, because there is only enough for a single load left in the box.

I don't know Delia's mother. I don't even know her name. But I take great care with her things, washing them without hurry or judgment because that is how I would want my Aunt Winnie to be taken care of if she was ever in such a situation to need this kind of help.

I take my time scrubbing the windowsills in the living room and kitchen, noting that there is grease and dust built up thick enough to need me to scrape it off in spots, instead of simply swiping it off with the rag and a little cleaning solution. No matter. I have too much on my mind to sit still anyway. I need something to do with my hands to keep my thoughts from turning down a dark path.

I suspected Frank of murder. I'm not sure I'm ready to forgive myself for that just yet. I am so glad that I was wrong on that front.

I take out the vacuum, making sure Delia's mother's door is closed while the old machine runs over the carpet. The whole room is in need of a thorough scrubbing. I know I should stop to take a break, but my hands are antsy for movement, to make recompense in some way for assuming the worst of a man who is clearly good to his core.

The walls are tacky to the touch in parts, and need a good washing, so I start on that task while my mind races.

Who could have done something so terrible as cutting off a woman's hand and hiding it in a cookie jar? Everyone in Sweetwater Falls is wonderful.

My shoulders slump when it dawns on me that there is possibly a larger scope to this investigation than just the residents of Sweetwater Falls. Anyone passing through could have used the charity drive as their dumping grounds for the sinister deed, and no one would be any the wiser. The criminal mastermind could be states away by now, laughing at how easy it was to get away with murder.

When Frank's footsteps slide down the hall toward me, the rag I've been scrubbing the walls with drops into the bucket. "Am I being too loud out here?"

The corner of Frank's mouth lifts. "Nah. I can't sleep in that rocking chair. Hurts my back. I've been going out to my car to sleep at night, actually. It's not the best, but the furniture here is too filthy to sit or sleep on."

"I can see that. But by the time Logan and I finish cleaning up, it won't be nearly as bad."

Frank runs his hands through his greasy black hair, letting the dim lamplight highlight the dark half-moons under his eyes. "If I haven't told you how grateful I am that you and Logan came here to check on Delia, and then stayed to help clean up the place, then let me say it again. Thank you for doing this, Cupcake Queen. I can't stand to see my sweet Delia all torn up. I'm trying to wrap my mind around how to help her mother."

"You're a good person, Frank." I want to ask him about the fishing trip he said he went on with Rip and Marcus, but I know there's no decent segue, so I lean on the late hour and skip to the information I need to know for my brain to settle. "Frank, when was the last time you went fishing?"

Frank takes my question as a nudge toward his brand

of self-care, casting a warm smile my way. "Two weekends ago? Something like that. I usually go with Rip and Marcus, but they couldn't make it, so I went by myself." He takes a deep inhale, as if the mix of putrid waste and cleaning solution can be blocked out by the memory of fresh lake air. "Sometimes you have to get away. I'm glad I did, because now I can be there for Delia with a clearer head." He holds out his hand. "Got an extra rag? I'll help with the walls."

I shake my head. "No way. You've been looking after them for days. It's my turn. You go rest. In fact, if you want to get a hotel room for yourself for the night so you can stretch out in a real bed, Logan and I can look after them for you tonight."

Frank runs his hand down his face. "No. Tempting, but no. I want to be close by, in case my sweet Delia needs anything."

Only Frank sees Delia as a sweet person. She's the town gossip and comes across a little more tart than anything else most days. I'm glad she has someone in her corner who sees the best in her, and who will sleep in his car if it means he gets to stay nearby.

I chew on my lower lip while I bid Frank goodnight and then get back to the walls, scrubbing as high as I can reach, all the way down to the floor.

The rag is a muddy brown by the time Logan gets back with the carpet shampooer, so I empty my bucket into the kitchen sink while Logan starts shampooing the carpet. I am grateful for the dim light, so I can't see how dank the water is in his machine.

Frank's been staying on top of the dishes, so there aren't any to wash. But when I open the refrigerator, I grimace and then spiral into a coughing fit. The food is rotting, uncovered, and many things have spilled and congealed at the bottom of the fridge. I can see why Frank and Delia have been ordering in. Best keep this thing shut.

However, I'm just worked up enough to decide that this is the thing that needs tackling next. Breathing through my mouth, I bring the trash can beside the refrigerator and discard one thing after the other. That part is easy because nothing is salvageable. Even the condiments that rarely expire are sticky to the touch from the various viscous foods that have spilled and spoiled in the fridge.

I take out the shelves and place them in the dishwasher, filling the thing before I turn it on and pray it gets out the months' worth of gunk that seems permanently stuck in place.

My arms are sore while I take my time scrubbing out the interior of the fridge, but the workout is exactly what my soul needs tonight. I want to work myself into exhaustion, otherwise I know my brain won't be able to shut off for sleep.

Logan taps my shoulder around two in the morning. "I think it's time we turn in, Miss Charlotte."

I blink up at him, bleary-eyed and tired. "Huh? But

there's nowhere to sleep, and I'm not finished. There's something spattered on the ceiling."

Logan takes my hand gently. "We can tackle the ceiling tomorrow. Let's take a note from Frank's book and sleep in your car. It's not the best, but a few hours will do us both some good."

I have arguments aplenty, but none of them come from a place of power or maturity. I don't want to sleep because I just don't wanna. I don't want to stop because I might stumble upon the identity of the real killer if only I stay awake and think a bit longer.

But part of me knows that none of that is rational, and logic has forsaken my tired bones. After washing my hands and face as best I can while Logan takes out the trash, my hand falls into his while we walk to my car.

When I purchased my red sedan, I did not picture myself sleeping in the seats. It's a thing of luck that the summer air isn't unbearably hot tonight, nor are we near a main road that proves particularly noisy. I close my eyes as I lean back the driver's seat all the way, groaning at my muscles that now have the space to complain about being overworked.

Logan reaches over and tucks a stray strawberry blonde curl behind my ear, then stretches out as best he can in the reclined passenger's seat. There are many things we could say to each other, but after seeing Delia's mother in such a state of decline, words seem trite when our hearts are this heavy. Logan holds my hand in the moonlight while we breathe the fresh air from the partially rolled windows. It's a heady difference, breathing in the fragrance of trees, grass and the occasional flower bush when contrasted with what we've been breathing for the past few hours.

"Goodnight, Mister Flowers," I mutter before my breathing begins to even out.

So quiet, I can barely hear it, Logan whispers, "Goodnight, Mrs. Flowers." Then he presses his lips to my knuckles before tucking my hand under my cheek.

And just like that, we fall asleep together under the stars.

19

A FRESH START

Neither Logan nor I are fans of sleeping in my car, but we keep our groaning to a minimum in the morning while we pick up breakfast and bring it to the others.

"I can't believe you two did all this. It's like a new home!" Delia gushes as she spears her order of pancakes at the newly scrubbed and cleared table. She shakes her head as if she can't understand why we would want to help her mother. "I still can't believe you came all the way here just to check on me. It's the nicest thing. And then you cleaned my mother's house?"

Delia's mother smiles at us with glassy eyes that appear to go in and out of focus. "Delia, eat up. You need to get to school before the bus leaves." Then she places her fragile hand atop mine. "Delia can't play this morning. She's got to go to school."

I swallow hard, unsure how to address the elephant in the room. I don't have the education to know if it's best to play along with the twists and turns of dementia, or if it is better to correct her and bring her to the present. Instead of acting out of miseducation, I decide to give her hand a little squeeze and change the subject. "You have a lovely home." And it's true. Now that there isn't filth everywhere, I can see that the carpet is a rosy, pink color. When Logan and I hung the cleaned curtains, we could see that they were off-white with pink flowers along the hem. The lamp doesn't look so forgotten, now that it's not covered in spiderwebs. The kitchen is brighter now, and the stench of garbage has lost its battle with the bleach, and even that isn't as pungent since Logan and I opened the rest of the windows to air out the house earlier this morning before everyone awoke.

Delia clears the table after we finish our breakfast, and then pulls me aside into the living room while Logan and Frank sit with Delia's mother. "We've got several doctor's appointments today for her, so this might be where we say goodbye for a few days." She pats her pocket. "I'll make sure to call Betty this time, though. Do you think you and her can feed my turtle and get the mail for another day or two?"

I wrap my arms around her frame. "As long as you need. Don't think on it another second. And if you want to take a break, you call me, and I'll come back up here. Whatever you need. Understood?"

Delia nods, her eyes watering after she pulls back. "Thank you. Truly. I didn't know how badly I needed not to see my childhood home like that until I woke up this morning and finally felt a shred of optimism. That's all I wanted. Just a scrap of sanity. Now I can focus on getting my mom the healthcare she needs, so this doesn't happen again."

I don't want to tell Delia that perhaps her mother shouldn't be living alone, and that no matter how good the doctors are, it most likely will happen again that her house is trashed if she is left to her own devices.

Logan and I are somber on the way home, talking mostly about how sad we are for Delia, and what we would do in that situation, if our parents took ill.

By the time we reach home, I feel as if my relationship with Logan has solidified into something I never guessed could be possible for me. It's stable, more than I knew I needed.

My shower feels like a gift from heaven, and I waste no time scrubbing the dirt and sweat from my body so I can start this day anew. When I come out with wet hair, clad in jean cut-offs and a white t-shirt, Aunt Winnie has a cup of iced coffee waiting for me. "I did my best to add enough sugar, but if you need more, the tub of frosting is in the fridge." She grimaces, still unable to reconcile how sweet I prefer my coffee on the occasions where caffeine is non-negotiable. "Karen needs to go home to get a few things, so

I'm going to pick her up and take her. Want me to pick anything up for you while I'm out?"

I blink at my great-aunt, who is ninety-one and just as peppy and together as she was when I was a little girl. I don't know how fortune decided that she gets to keep her memories, and Delia's mother's memories have to fade. It makes me appreciate her that much more this morning. In lieu of answering my great-aunt's question, I cross the kitchen and throw my arms around her neck, hugging her close so we never slip away from each other. "I love you," I tell her, making sure that if all else fades, she will cling to that one truth.

Aunt Winnie chuckles. "I love you, honey cake. Betty called this morning and told me about what you did for Delia's mother. I'm so glad you're mine."

"I'm so glad you're mine," I echo, and it couldn't be more true. I am wholly hers, hoping to one day take after her lively spirit and charge boldly into any challenge that might come my way. I kiss her cheek and then take a sip of the iced coffee she made that, indeed, does not have enough sweetness for me to stomach an entire mug of the stuff.

Aunt Winnie reaches for the key to the golf cart and then pauses with a frown. "I know Karen needs me to pick her up, and we'll be only gone half an hour or so, but I worry about Janet being alone with Charles, even for that long."

My posture straightens. "You think he'll be mean to her the second Karen leaves?"

Aunt Winnie nods. "I don't want her to get the brunt of a bad day when we're trying to help her."

I raise my hand to volunteer. "I'm guessing he won't want his bad behavior witnessed. How about I go with you and stay with Janet and Rachel while you take Karen home? Then Janet has backup."

Aunt Winnie brightens. "Oh, would you? I hate to ask. You barely slept."

"I offered. Plus, I was going to feed Delia's turtle today, so Betty doesn't have to, and take in the mail."

"Are you sure?"

"I'm sure. Plus, I kind of hope I get to see Karen ordering around Charles again. Music to my ears."

Aunt Winnie chortles. "She's something else. Thanks, dear. And can you grab this chicken pot pie for me? I made two yesterday—one for us and one for Janet, so she has a night off from cooking. It's hard to get things done with an infant."

"Absolutely. That was nice of you." I take the pot pie and set it on my lap when I sit in the passenger's seat of Aunt Winnie's gold cart. I glance at my red sedan, recalling how sweet Logan looked when he slept there, his mouth lolled open, and his sandy blond hair mussed against the seat. Even when we're exhausted, he is still kind to me. He even texts me on my way to Karen's to tell me it was the worst night of sleep he's had in a long time, but he'd do it all over again if it meant we got to be together.

I kind of love the sappy nature of our relationship lately and wouldn't have it any other way.

When we pull into Janet's driveway in my Aunt Winnie's golf cart, there isn't the faintest sound of Charles yelling, which is quite the relief. I don't know much about marriage, but I do know I don't want to marry someone like Charles.

Karen kisses my cheek when we enter the surprisingly calm house. "Two for one? I didn't realize we were getting Charlotte and you, Winnie."

I hold out my hands for Rachel, to give Janet a break from holding her baby. "I'm here to hang out with Janet while you go pick up your things with Aunt Winnie. How long do you think you're staying here?"

Janet answers for Karen. "For as long as she possibly can. I love having you here, Karen. The whole place feels different."

Karen winks at Janet. "That's called breathing, dear. You're breathing finally. It's addictive. I highly recommend."

I glance around. "Where's Charles?"

Janet taps her foot to the floor. "Hiding downstairs. Karen told him to clear the dishes after lunch, and he refused. He's been hiding down there ever since."

"He'll poke his head out eventually." Karen gives me a serious look. "Don't you dare do those dishes, and don't let

Janet do them, either. She made lunch; it's only fair that Charles does the dishes. It's called teamwork."

I snicker at the lesson Karen is bent on teaching the obstinate grown man. "I love you so much."

"That's because you're sensible." Karen's nose lifts as she exits with Aunt Winnie, closing the door behind her.

I fix Janet with a scandalous grin. "I want every single detail."

But before Janet can tell me all about her time with Karen, I hear Charles stomping up the steps from the basement. "Is she gone?"

I answer in a sing-song voice that makes it clear he is still to be on his best behavior. "Hi, Charles. I'm here to visit my new friend and her baby. I don't know you all that well. I'm Charlotte, Winifred's niece."

He grumbles at me, since I clearly don't have the same commanding presence as Karen. "Fine." He stomps away like a child in lieu of a proper greeting.

I quirk an eyebrow at Janet while I rock Rachel in my arms. "He's awfully cheerful today."

Janet grimaces. "He's mad because Karen makes him mind his manners. And he's been wanting to get up into the attic, but he doesn't want to pull out the ladder while Karen is here. Probably afraid she'll make him polish the ladder or something."

I snicker at the thought. "What does he need from the attic?"

Janet shrugs. "He just said he wants all his stuff out of

there because I can't be trusted not to donate his things. So, everything, I guess. You don't have to do it. I could only reach the box of stuff near the entrance. The ladder isn't all that helpful because it's only got three steps to it."

I beam at her, handing over the baby. "Point me in the right direction. I'm taller than the both of you. I can get his stuff down."

Janet takes in my superior height as if this is a new observation. "Really? Thank you! It's one of those situations where both of us can only reach the opening, so we either grab what's at the opening and that's all, or we shove things toward the back and intend never to be able to reach them again."

"Not a problem."

Janet sniffs Rachel's midsection. "I need to change Rachel's diaper. The ladder's in the hall closet, and the attic entrance is right at the end of the hall just over there." She motions to the hallway to the left of the front door and then meanders toward the right, where I'm assuming Rachel's bedroom lies.

I follow her instructions and ready myself to help clean out my second house in as many days. No matter. It's easy to get out the ladder and make myself useful. I don't mind pulling out the first few bags of things that feel like clothes with something hard mixed in—perhaps shoes. But the rest of the things are harder to reach, so I balance one foot on the top step of the stool, and the other on the raised handle, tipping precariously so I can pull my whole body up into the attic to better see what it is I'm dealing with. I peek into the attic to make sure there's enough space for me to crouch, so I don't hoist myself onto something of value and accidentally break it.

But nothing could have prepared me for the sight that greets me.

Instead of odds and ends that could be donated or thrown away, a human leg wrapped in plastic fills my vision before the ladder goes out from under me, sending me tumbling to the floor below.

20

ATTIC ATTACK

*M*y scream doesn't hold back, nor does the ground when my chin smacks to the floor with a loud bang. My ankle feels unsteady, like I twisted it in the ladder on my way down.

I don't expect that anything other than poor balance made me fall, but when I gaze up at Charles, who is standing over me with wild eyes and his fists clenched, I realize I read this situation all wrong.

"What are you doing in my attic?" he seethes, looking as if he is on the verge of coming unhinged.

I decide not to answer him. Letting him know that I saw a human leg wrapped in plastic in his attic probably isn't the best thing to tell him in this moment where I am at a clear disadvantage. "Did you kick out the ladder from under me while I was trying to help your wife get your things down from the attic for you?"

My sidestep of the obvious doesn't pass muster as he fixates on my face, his upper lip curled. "This is my house, and I don't want you in it!"

Janet rushes to us with Rachel in her arms. "Charles, don't yell at Charlotte! She was only helping." I'm glad that Janet can correct his bad behavior, though it seems she can only do this for others, and not to stand up for herself.

He whirls on her, his voice booming so loud that I flinch. "Get out of here!"

Rachel is spooked and starts to howl with fright at the angry man.

Janet whimpers, holding her baby tight to her chest. "Let's go, Charlotte. Did you fall?"

"Charles kicked the ladder from beneath me."

Janet's indignant inhale does nothing to diffuse the situation. "I can't believe you did that to her!"

"Get out!" Charles shouts again, making his wife wince while his nostrils flare.

Janet's lower lip quivers while Rachel cries. "Let's go outside, Charlotte. Get you some air and see if you're okay."

"I'm alright." Though as I try to stand, pain shoots through my leg, making my bold declaration questionable. I can't put a lick of pressure on my left leg, and somehow, I need to get past the angry man in the middle of the hallway, who seems intent on not letting me pass.

"You're not going anywhere," Charles informs me. He

glowers while I hobble to the wall to lean against it. Then over his shoulder to Janet, he hisses. "Out."

Though I don't want to be alone with Charles, knowing what I know, the need to keep Rachel and Janet safe is far more acute. I lock eyes with Janet and nod, trying to assure us both that I've got everything under control, and that there's no need to worry. It's a hard sell, given that concern is causing sweat to break out on my forehead and upper lip, and I can't even stand without the help of the wall.

Fear rounds Janet's eyes as she runs out of the house with Rachel in her arms.

My shoulders lower in relief, knowing the baby won't be hurt in Charles' path of rage.

Only I am caught in his crosshairs. I decide not to play dumb anymore, since he clearly isn't buying the act. "If you turn yourself in, they'll be more likely to work with you, Charles."

"Turn myself in? Turn myself in?" He grabs at his dark hair and tugs on the strands, making him look that much more deranged. "Do you have any idea what it's like to have a mother who never does a thing you say? Do you know what it's like to hear that shrill voice telling you that you have to figure out a way to pay the bills without her help?"

My expression sours. "You murdered your mother because she wouldn't financially support you as an adult? Are you joking with this?"

It is clearly the wrong thing to say, but after watching

Delia break down over her mother's plight and being able to do nothing about it other than clean her house, I cannot stomach this spoiled brat of a man who took for granted that he cannot scream his way out of every problem in life.

Charles' upper lip curls. "You have no idea how expensive it is to have a family. Diapers aren't free, you know! And Janet's no help, saying she can't find a job that would allow her to have the baby with her there. Not like I can watch the baby while I'm at work!"

I pinch the bridge of my nose, trying to summon sanity to surface. "So, your only course of action was that you had to kill your mother? That solved it all?"

Charles' voice quiets. "It got her to shut up, didn't it?"

A chill runs over my skin, causing goosebumps to break out all over my arms. "You should have confessed when I found your mother's hand in the cookie jar at the charity drive. Things will go so much worse for you if you don't come clean with the police now. You still have choices, Charles! Make the right choice for once."

Perhaps adding "for once" isn't helping my situation, but in fairness, my ankle hurts so badly, I can hardly see straight. I need something to grip, to hold onto so I don't put weight on my ankle and fall.

Charles takes a step toward me with murder in his eyes. "You've seen too much. You know I can't let you leave here."

I will not back down. I will not let him see me cower and cry, even though that is all I want to do. He is used to

Janet cowering. He is used to getting what he wants by being bigger, louder and meaner. I have no interest in playing that game. I don't know when it was that I went from dormouse to lion, but I think it was shortly after I moved to Sweetwater Falls and had women teaching me how glorious it feels to live without the constant stream of insecurity closing my mouth and stifling my dreams.

Janet deserves better than this. Rachel cannot grow to think that this is how men should behave.

The very act of a woman standing without backing down is something I can tell that Charles is unaccustomed to. He doesn't know what to do when I stare at him, seething without a hint of fear.

Little does he know that I *am* afraid; I just won't let him see it.

I'm afraid he will overpower me easily, injured as I am.

I'm afraid that Janet will never understand that this is wrong, and she doesn't have to stand for it.

I'm afraid that I will not live through this altercation to feel my great-aunt's arms around me ever again.

Her last hug for me was a good one, so I hold that love tight in my heart and use it to propel me forward. "You're turning yourself in, Charles."

But the man does not understand that I will never back down, now that I have the strength of a collection of fierce women flowing through my veins. "If you struggle, I'll make this so much more painful for you."

Charles takes a step to block me and then lunges. He

knocks me back against the wall at the end of the hallway and kicks at my bum ankle.

Pain ricochets up my leg so acute that I cannot work air into my lungs to force out a scream. A savage need to protect Janet and Rachel is the only focal point in my mind, overriding any fear that might get behind the wheel. My hands raise up to grip onto his face, using that as my anchor to keep me upright. My fingers dig into his eyes, my mouth pulled in an expression of horror that might haunt me to the end of my days. I don't want to be doing this. I don't want to know that my hands are capable of hurting someone so gruesomely.

I also don't want someone like Charles roaming the streets of my precious small town that has so thoroughly captivated my heart.

Charles cries out and falls back, giving me time to escape. I hobble down the hallway and grab up my purse so I can call for help the second I hit the free air. But the moment I throw open the front door, relief floods my veins. The help I was going to call for has already arrived.

JANET'S NEW LIFE

*D*elia's house across the street from the scene of the crime has become a haven for Janet, Rachel and me after Logan and his father arrest Charles for everything he's done. Wayne, Logan's partner, is still bagging up the evidence from the crawl space. Fortunately, they didn't ask for my help in retrieving the body parts, so I've been able to rest my sore ankle from the comfort of Delia's couch while I watched Logan march a handcuffed Charles into the back of his squad car.

Karen rocks Rachel beside me, while Janet sits in front of the unlit fireplace, staring blankly as she fights to process all that's gone wrong in such a short time. Karen's voice is soft while Aunt Winnie paces back and forth in front of the picture window, taking in details just as I am. "Charles doesn't deserve your tears, Janet."

It's then that Janet finally pries her gaze from the

hearth, bewildered at Karen's statement. "I'm not crying for him. These are tears of relief. I'm free, Karen. I'm finally free."

Her lightened spirit washes over all of us, allowing my shoulders to relax into the cushions.

"I don't know what to do now, though," Janet admits. "I don't know how to get a job where I can keep Rachel with me. I don't know how I could possibly make enough to keep the house."

Aunt Winnie stops her pacing. "Do you want to keep the house?"

Janet pauses, tilting her head to consider the question. "Not really, but we need a place to live." She pinches the bridge of her nose. "I've pictured myself leaving a hundred times over. But now that it's really happening, I don't know how to put one foot in front of the other."

Karen and Aunt Winnie lock eyes, and Karen nods like a pioneer woman readying to blaze a new trail. Then she turns her chin toward Janet. "You can start by moving in with me. You and Rachel. You won't pay rent, so you won't have big expenses."

My mouth falls open in wonder. My heart fills with a hope so powerful, my lungs feel as if they are filling with helium, my posture lifting. My mind begins to race, now that it has been given a more positive direction in which to spend my focus. "If you need money for normal day-to-day things and you can handle yourself with a spatula, you can bake cupcakes with Betty and me. Rachel's always welcome to come along and be our junior baker."

Aunt Winnie's eyes are damp with emotion. "And I can watch our little baby angel anytime you like."

Janet gapes at me. "You don't even know if I can bake. You're offering me a job, just like that?"

A soft smile finds my face even as I readjust the icepack on my ankle. "I can teach you to bake. It wouldn't be your forever job. Just something until you get your legs under you again."

Janet's hand cups a quiet cry when it comes out in the form of gratitude. "Thank you." Then she turns to Karen, seeing the thin, wiry warrior in the same way I do—as a beacon of strength and hope that the world so desperately needs. "You want us to come live with you?"

Karen rocks Rachel—two angels clinging to each other after a storm. "I can't think of anything better. I admit, I'm mildly jealous that Agnes has Marianne in her life, and Winifred has Charlotte in her home. I'd like to shake things up a little. Infuse a bit of life into my home. See what sort of magic happens when I open my life to someone new." She gives Rachel a sweet kiss on her round forehead. "Maybe *two* new someones."

Though my ankle is in agony, I still feel as if I could get up and dance with how happy I am, now that things are falling into place for Janet. It's not the best way to escape a bad situation, and there are certainly quite a few question marks in her future, but for once she actually gets to look forward to a life here in Sweetwater Falls, surrounded by some of the best women I know.

When Rachel begins to fuss, Janet takes her baby from Karen and cradles her tight to her chest. "I didn't know I could have options. I didn't know this sort of thing was possible."

Karen beams up at Janet. "Honey, with the right people in your corner, anything is possible."

22

THE CHARITY DRIVE

*S*ome of my favorite moments in life happen at the events held in Sweetwater Falls, and today is no exception. Everyone, it seems, has turned out for the charity drive, whose purpose is to raise money for the local food bank. Marianne and I have our black vendor aprons around our waists and oversized pins on our white t-shirts, announcing to the customers that "It's for charity, so haggle at your own risk."

The townsfolk are lined up at the door, and many have already started picnicking on blankets on the grass while they munch on hot dogs. Everyone chats animatedly while a group of high school students plays lively music off to the side.

I don't have the wherewithal to run a cash register with this many people filtering in and out. I don't know how

Marianne does it. She has hawk-like focus paired with the patience of a saint. I am content to hand out shopping bags and greet the people coming in to shop till they drop. Frankly, that's my favorite part—seeing all the people I love and making sure they know they are welcome.

Kurt beams at me as he takes the bag and the piece of taffy I hand to him. "Now that I'm not searching for my lost wedding ring, I can actually enjoy this event." He holds up his hand to display the treasure to me. "It wasn't even here! It dropped onto the floor of the bathroom at home." He rolls his eyes at the folly.

My hand rests over my heart. "Oh, thank goodness! I'm glad you found it." No wonder he didn't want to announce what it was he'd lost. His wedding ring from his late wife is something he wouldn't want to have misplaced.

When I catch sight of Delia and Frank in the line, I wave energetically at them, handing them each a bag and a freshly wrapped piece of homemade pink taffy when they get to the front of the line. It's then that I see they have Delia's mother beside them with her walker. She's so stooped and short that I couldn't see her until she was standing directly in front of me. "Hi, guys! Glad to see you. I didn't know you'd be bringing your mother to Sweet-water Falls."

Though, I should have guessed as much. It was either bring her here or Delia move there to look after her. The woman really shouldn't be living alone.

Delia's mother regards me with kind but unfocused eyes. "Hello, young lady. I'm Gladys. This is my lovely daughter, Delia. Not Delilah. Delia. People get that confused sometimes."

I don't point out that we've met, nor that I stayed in her house not too long ago. I reach out my hand to rest on hers, which is clutching her walker. "Good morning, Gladys. My, that's a lovely shawl. Did you knit that?"

Gladys beams at me. "I did. Years ago, back when my Delia was a little girl. But it's timeless. Never goes out of style."

"I can see that." And she's right. It's a soft teal that could almost be in the cream color family. "It's nice to meet you, Gladys. I'm Charlotte."

Frank hooks a thumb in his belt loop. "You'll be seeing Charlotte a lot more often, Gladys, now that you're moving in with Delia."

Gladys' brows crease, and then she smiles. "Oh, that's right. My home is different now. You should come and see it. We've got a turtle!"

Delia offers me a tired smile. "We sure do. Thanks for helping Betty look after Michelangelo while I was gone."

I'm holding up the line, but this hug cannot wait a second longer. I throw my arms around Delia, knowing the emotional strain on her must be acute. It's hard to watch someone you love suffer, and forget the details of a life you need them to remember to make yours seem like it truly happened. "I'm happy to stop by and help out however I can," I whisper to Delia.

Delia squeezes me tight, her frizzy chestnut hair trapping itself in my mouth when the wind shifts our way. "Thank you. Frank has been my knight in shining armor. He's practically got my mom all moved into my spare bedroom. He never tires. I don't know how he does it."

"He loves you. That's what you do for someone you love. You show up, ready to help." I reach over and squeeze Frank's wrist.

"That's right," Frank echoes. "Whatever my sweet ladies need, I'll see to. Right, Gladys?"

Gladys lights up when I pull back from Delia's hug. "Oh, yes. Did you know that our Frank has his own newsstand? He reads me the paper every night. Such a good boy."

Frank smiles at me, and warmth fills my heart as I hand them shopping bags and wish them well in the maze of tables laden with items ready to be brought to new homes.

My gaze catches on Karen, who is pushing a stroller with Rachel buckled inside, cooing at the little girl who has brought so much newness of life to us all. Janet reaches over to adjust Rachel's blanket at the same time that Gladys reaches to Delia to tuck a lock of hair behind her daughter's ear. The visual fills me with a hug that reaches all the way to my insides.

"You're supposed to be resting your ankle," Betty reminds me as she sidles up beside me, hooking her arm through mine. "That chair Rip set out for you isn't a decoration, I hope you realize."

I frown down at the brace on my foot, wishing I could escape all the bad things and live only in the moments where mothers dote on their daughters, and all is well with the world. "I'm alright."

"Don't think I'm above tattling on you to Winifred. I'll bet she'll have something to say about you ignoring doctor's orders. Rip had you manning the front door because he knew that was a job you could do sitting down."

"He's a good guy."

Betty bumps her hip to mine. "He sure is. I nabbed myself one of the best." She jerks her chin toward Janet. "The new girl starts baking with us tomorrow. Do you think she's up for it?"

I smile at Janet, admiring her courage after making it through such a rough few years of her marriage. "I think she can handle anything that comes her way. And when she can't, she's got us to help out."

Betty pats my cheek before she waves to her husband across the way. "Can't imagine anything better."

And just like that, Betty jogs into the throngs of shoppers, her smile mixing in with the others who have come together just for fun.

For each other.

For this sweet small town, where anything can happen.

The End.

Love the book? Leave a review!

23

KEY LIME CUPCAKE RECIPE

Yield: 12 Cupcakes

Happiness sweeps through me while I take in the wonder that I was hoping she would experience. "Forty-nine years deserves a celebration with something sweet. It's a key lime cupcake with a key lime whipped cream frosting. Graham cracker crumbles on top."

-Key Lime Killer, by Molly Maple

 or the Cupcake:

½ CUP UNSALTED BUTTER AT ROOM TEMPERATURE

¾ cup granulated sugar

¼ cup whole milk

¼ cup cream cheese

2 eggs at room temperature

1 tsp pure vanilla extract

1 Tbsp key lime juice (lime juice can be used as a substitution)

1 ½ cups all-purpose flour

1 tsp baking powder

½ tsp salt

3-4 drops green food coloring, if preferred

Instructions for the Cupcake:

1. Preheat the oven to 350°F.
2. Using a stand mixer, cream at medium-low speed ½ cup unsalted butter and ¾ cup granulated sugar in a large mixing bowl until well combined.
3. Mix in ¼ cup whole milk and ¼ cup cream cheese.
4. Add eggs one at a time and beat on medium speed until well combined.

5. Add 1 tsp pure vanilla extract and 1 Tbsp key lime juice. Mix until well combined.

6. In a medium bowl, sift together 1 ½ cups all-purpose flour, 1 tsp baking powder, and ½ tsp salt. Add to wet ingredients and mix on medium speed until well combined. Mix in green food coloring, if preferred.

7. Divide the batter into your 12-count lined cupcake pan, filling each one 2/3 the way full.

8. Bake for 15-20 minutes at 350°F, or until a toothpick inserted in the center comes out clean.

9. Let them cool in the pan for 10 minutes, then transfer to a cooling rack. Cool to room temperature before frosting.

INGREDIENTS FOR THE KEY LIME WHIPPED CREAM **Frosting:**

1 ½ CUP HEAVY WHIPPING CREAM

1/3 cup confectioner's sugar

1/2 tsp vanilla extract

1 Tbsp key lime juice (can use lime juice as substitution)

Optional: graham cracker crumbs to sprinkle on top

. . .

INSTRUCTIONS FOR THE KEY LIME WHIPPED CREAM
Frosting:

1. Beat 1 ½ cup heavy cream with 1/3 cup confectioner's sugar in a stand mixer until fluffy (3-4 minutes on medium-high speed).
2. Add ½ tsp vanilla extract and 1 Tbsp key lime juice. Mix until fluffy.

TIP: LOOKS BEST WHEN SCOOPED WITH AN ICE CREAM SCOOP, then leveled, and placed atop a cooled cupcake. Then sprinkle with graham cracker crumbs.

24

FREE PREVIEW

Enjoy a free preview of *Lemon Lawlessness*, book eleven in the Cupcake Crimes series.

Lemon Lawlessness

"*C*harlotte McKay, how much do you love me?" Fisher says in lieu of a greeting. He's barely emerged from the kitchen, and I can already see by the sweat dotting his forehead that he's worried he has wandered too far from where he is needed most.

"I love you a whole lot of much," I reply without missing a beat. Though the lace doilies and collection of teapots on the shelf are perfectly in place and the atmosphere of the dining room in The Snuggle Inn is serene and cozy, Fisher is a ball of anxiety. I shift in my seat, rearranging my pink cloth napkin atop the starched white tablecloth.

He wrings his hands, then scratches at the thick black hair on his arms. "I'm shorthanded today. Can I bribe you with free dinners for you and Winifred for the week if you come back into the kitchen to help me out?"

Even though my feet are tired from all the work I did in my cupcake bakery this morning, my smile is bright when it is aimed at my dear friend and fellow food enthusiast. "You can bribe me with a hug, and I would've accepted that as payment." I glance around the dining room, noting that there is only a dozen or so people sitting at the tables, which doesn't seem nearly enough to warrant the panic and sweat wafting off Fisher as he runs his fingers through his slick inky curls to pull them away from his rounded face.

Fisher values fresh, handmade pasta as much as I adore the excitement of a new cupcake flavor. If he's having trouble in the kitchen, there are few people he trusts more than me to help him remedy that roadblock.

I do not take that privilege for granted. Ever since I moved to the small town of Sweetwater Falls nearly a year ago to live with my great-aunt Winifred, I have been fortunate enough to make several friends—more than I've had in my life, actually. It feels good to know Fisher understands he can count on me to help when he's frazzled.

Even though I've been on my feet since before the sun rose, I get a second wind just for Fisher that lifts me to stand so I can wrap my arms around his sturdy frame. "Let's do this," I tell him, determination plain on my features.

Fisher exhales as if he is readying to cry. He squeezes me around the ribs with his giant forearms. He's burly, with a small hint of a belly puffing over the apron wound about his waist. "Thank you, Charlotte." He talks animatedly as we walk toward the kitchen, explaining what needs to be done. "It's the Ketchup Committee," he says as if I should know what that means. "They need an assortment of meatballs, breads and fries for their sampling, which is fine, but they were supposed to come tomorrow, not tonight. I have my regular menu I need to prep for tonight, but the dining room is fully booked all evening long, so it's more than the usual workload. And of course, my sous chef is sick, so it's all on me."

My lower lip juts out as I flip my blonde curls over my shoulder. "He is? What's Nathan got? That flu that's been going around?" I shake my head. "I've been washing my hands like crazy to make sure I don't bring anything in the house to spread to Aunt Winnie."

My ninety-one-year-old, five-foot tall great-aunt never seems fragile, but I don't like to roll the dice with the person who is most precious in the world to me. Just yesterday, Aunt Winnie, Agnes and Karen were out in the middle of the woods birdwatching for so long, I worried they'd lost their way. Then when they came home, they were winded and tightlipped about their afternoon, carrying a basket I wasn't allowed to touch, which has given me pause ever since.

With the kookie three members of the Live Forever Club, a rose is never just a rose, and birdwatching is never just birdwatching.

I'm still waiting for the other shoe to drop on that one.

Fisher pushes the kitchen door for me, escorting me into his home away from home. "I have no idea what Nathan's got, but I do know that I'm shorthanded on a day where I really can't afford to be pulled in multiple directions."

I glance around the kitchen and notice that Fisher's usual cleanly organizational standard has gone the way of creative chaos. I grimace at the pots overflowing in the sink, the sauce that's boiled over and stained the stovetop and counter, and the smell of liver that permeates my nose without my permission. "Oh, Fish. This is... You should have called me. I would have come straightaway."

Fisher casts around the kitchen hopelessly. "I lost my phone in the mess somewhere." He motions to an opened gift basket of mini muffins. "Help yourself. Someone gifted them to us, apparently, but I'm not all that hungry. Nathan ate half the basket yesterday. They're pretty stale today. Plus, they smell weird." He lifts starched white dish towels from the edge of the basket that the muffins came wrapped in. "Nice gift, but I'm too overwhelmed to appreciate anything today."

"I'm good."

Fisher makes an executive decision and tosses the day-old mini muffins in the garbage to have one less thing to deal with. Then he throws the white dish towels the muffins were wrapped in down into the dirty linens bin. He scratches his arm distractedly, his eyes casting around the kitchen

"Put me to work." I slap my palms together, readying to tackle the madness and turn it into mastery. "Okay, then. I'm going to start by cleaning up, and you focus on the dinner tonight."

"But I have to deal with the rest of the lunch rush first!" he protests, sweat dotting his forehead and upper lip.

I shake my head. "Lunch just got a lot simpler. Soup and sandwiches," I declare as I glance into the soup pot on the stove and guestimate that it will suffice for the next two hours.

"But what about the dinner menu I had planned?" he frets. "And I need to prep the salmon for tomorrow's dinner."

"Not happening." I step back out into the dining area and inform the waitstaff of the menu changes. If we're going to stay on top of it all and bust out a dinner that will wow the guests, we have to scale back somewhere. When I return to the kitchen, Fisher still looks lost, which isn't how he ever appears while he's in his happy place. I pat his shoulder, straightening my five-foot-ten posture with confidence I try to will myself to feel. "We can do this. One thing at a time, though. I'm cleaning, and you're prepping the dinner. When the lunch orders come in, we'll deal with them in the simplest way we can. We're scaling back to sandwiches for lunch so we can put out the dinner you had planned. Got it?"

Fisher swallows hard but doesn't remember how to move from his spot until I grab up a rag and cleaning solution and go to town on the counter beside the stove. That seems to set his feet into motion. "Dinner is going to be liver stroganoff, potato and turnip medallions with braised carrots, arugula salad with strawberries, and a lemon crème brûlée."

"Sounds like a plan." I don't look up from the spot where I am cleaning because I know that if I do, I will be overwhelmed with the work ahead of me.

Scrub the counters. That's the only job.

Once I finish that, I move to the dishes, which are intimidating to tackle. Still, I keep my focus on one thing at a time, reminding myself that it can and will get done because it has to.

Gotta love a commercial dishwasher. I notice that with every load that comes through and is put away, Fisher's stress seems to diminish by a few degrees. Once he can move his elbows without knocking into a dirty dish, his shoulders lower and he doesn't look as if he's going to cry.

After the dishes, I tackle as many of the appliances as I can, sticking to the ones that aren't in use while Fisher begins to worry aloud. "There will be twice as many people as last year for the event tonight, by the way. You wouldn't think a ketchup committee needs more members added, but as it turns out, they can't make decisions without double the amount of people."

"Explain to me this Ketchup Committee. Is there a Mustard Brigade that comes in after them?"

Fisher blinks at me, not registering my joke. "I always forget that you haven't lived in Sweetwater Falls even a year yet. You seem like you've always been one of us. I can't imagine not knowing you."

I press my hand to my heart, savoring the compliment. "Same."

Fisher chops the liver into small chunks, but the way he does it is with skillful care, like an artist approaching a canvas. "The Ketchup Committee is exactly what it sounds like. Once a year, they decide on new flavors, marketing strategies, and what's new in ketchup."

I open my mouth but then close it, so I don't say something stupid. I can't imagine what could possibly be new in ketchup. "Interesting," I lie, grateful, not for the first time, that my life's trajectory led me to be a cupcake baker, and not a ketchup enthusiast.

"I'm nervous," Fisher admits. "Every year, they come here, and every year, I chicken out."

"On what?"

Fisher keeps his eyes on the cutting board while he speaks. "One of my dreams is to have my homemade ketchup tasted and tested by the Ketchup Committee, but they're so self-important and stuffy that I get nervous and start mumbling. I chicken out every single year. I told myself that this year would be different. I even called Eugene's restaurant to ask if I could enter my ketchup for judging. Eugene is the founder of the Ketchup Committee. Owns a French restaurant in Hamshire. I asked his head chef to pass along my request, but I never heard back." He coats the liver pieces with seasoned flour in a mixing bowl, tossing them with a few flicks of his wrist. "I don't know why tonight should be any different than the other years where I chickened out. There are double the judges this year. No way will I go for it with that much pressure."

I scoff. "No way am I letting you back down, now that I know that little tidbit." I channel Aunt Winnie, feeling her brash confidence in my bones. I might not always be able to be brave for myself, but for my friends, I won't back down.

Fisher and I work in tandem until the kitchen is spotless, lunch is served, dinner is prepped, the tasting samples are made, and there's nothing left to do but work on the lemon crème brûlée together as the afternoon turns into early evening.

Lenny rushes into the kitchen, his eyes wide. "They're here! Every one of them with their noses in the air, too. You'd think they're sampling gold, the way they parade around, demanding more than we have to offer." The man in his forties is always wearing a white dress shirt and navy trousers while on the clock. His black hair is slicked to the side with a bit too much gel. Lenny carries himself with the self-importance that befits his position as the owner of The Snuggle Inn even as he harrumphs. "I'm telling you, Fisher, they're going to be finicky tonight. Tell me you have a dinner that will stop their highfalutin nitpicking."

Fisher goes pale, scratching at his arm while I cook the eggs into a custard over a double boiler.

I answer for my friend. "This dinner is going to knock their socks off," I assure Lenny.

Lenny nods once. "Well, they're setting up for the sampling, so let's get this show on the road. The event comes first, then their dinner."

Fisher and I have the trays of things to dip in ketchup ready to go. It's the foggy jar of ketchup on the counter beside the trays that Fisher is nervous about. He reaches for the jar, shaking his head as he makes to put it back in the fridge.

I step in because there is no way that this is not happening, whether Fisher is ready to put himself out there or not. I grab up a tray of tasting samples, then wait until Fisher moseys to the sink to wash up. I keep my movements quiet when I snatch the homemade ketchup jar from the fridge. I toss my hair back, donning a confident smile that demands attention as I walk into the dining room that is positively packed. I might not always be able to ask for what I want out of life, but the moment one of my friends makes their goals known, I'm ready to spring into action to help make their dreams come true.

The waitstaff brought in more chairs than the fire inspector would approve of to accommodate the crowd of taste testers. The containers of ketchup in question are all lined up on a long table on the side of the room, so I make a show of setting out the sampling bites of meatballs, bread cubes and fries in between each offering.

Though each jar is numbered, I set Fisher's homemade creation before Jar Number One and unscrew the lid.

I don't mean to grimace. I'm certainly not a ketchup aficionado. But something is very wrong with Fisher's ketchup. I debate taking it straight back to the kitchen and blame it on performance anxiety. Whatever this is, I don't think it's ketchup. It's reddish, but the wrong shade. It doesn't coat the jar but runs down the sides—too thin to spread on a burger with any real confidence it wouldn't slip right off. And it doesn't smell right. There's not a hint of tang or tomato that hits my nose when I unscrew the top and label it "Mystery Ketchup" on a piece of paper in hopes that encourages curiosity.

Quick as I can, I move to the back of the dining area, making myself scarce as the Ketchup King (as so declared on his name tag that's stuck onto his suit's lapel) explains the rating system everyone is to use.

I stand at the kitchen door, watching with bated breath as the first few people congregate around the mystery jar, poking meatballs and scraps of bread onto their plates as they ladle Fisher's offering and others into their tasting bowls.

It happens slowly at first, but then spreads throughout the first dozen tasters. It's a grimace, a blanche, then a sniff at the tasting bowl, followed by outrage. "Is this some sort of joke?" one of them demands to know. "What is this?"

Another person with the name tag reading "Archie" turns gaunt. He's squat and has barely any neck to him. His caramel-colored tuft of hair is combed over his bald spot that looks to be rapidly attempting to take over his whole head. "It's... That's not ketchup!" He touches his finger to the surface, then sniffs it like dog, as if expecting he can get every ingredient's complete history from scent alone. "It's blood! He just put someone's blood in his mouth!"

Then the person next to Archie who just tasted Fisher's ketchup turns and vomits on the floor in wide dramatic puddles while Lenny runs to the table to see what went wrong. Archie runs into the kitchen, I'm guessing to wash the sick off his shoes, the blood off his finger, and any other trace that marks this as the worst ketchup tasting of his life.

The Ketchup King marches to the table to inspect the mystery jar. "Who put this here? This isn't in the official entries." Eugene's voice turns sharp. "Who did this?"

Panic dries my throat so that when I raise my hand, my voice comes out a croak. "I did. It's homemade ketchup."

The Ketchup King takes a tiny sample on his tongue,

swirling it around as if he is sipping wine. His face sours, and then he shoves three meatballs in his mouth. "Blood!" he accuses, pointing his finger at me. "Arrest this woman! She's feeding us blood!"

I back into the wall, hoping to fade from sight, but as everyone turns to shout at me, I can see the damage is done.

My attempt to make Fisher's dreams come true has seriously backfired.

Read *Lemon Lawlessness* today!

ABOUT THE AUTHOR

Author Molly Maple believes in the magic of hot tea and the romance of rainy days.

She is a fan of all desserts, but cupcakes have a special place in her heart. Molly spends her days searching for fresh air, and her evenings reading in front of a fireplace.

Molly Maple is a pen name for USA Today bestselling fantasy author Mary E. Twomey, and contemporary romance author Tuesday Embers.

Visit her online at www.MollyMapleMysteries.com. Sign up for her newsletter to be alerted when her next new release is coming.

Made in the USA
Monee, IL
30 December 2022